YOU KNOW I

need you

WILLOW WINTERS

I married the bad boy from Brooklyn.

The one with the tattoos and the look in his eyes that told me he was bad news.

The kind of look that comes with all sorts of warnings.

I knew what I was doing.

I knew by the way he first held me that he would be my downfall; how he owned me with his forceful touch.

I couldn't say no to him, not that I wanted to. That was then, and it seems like forever ago.

Years later, I've grown up and moved on. But he's still the man I married. Dangerous in ways I don't like to think about and tried to ignore for so long.

I did this to myself. I knew better than to fall for him.

I only wish love were enough to fix this …

You Know I Need You is book 2 of the second duet in the You Are Mine series. Book 1, *You Know I Love You*, must be read first for this duet.

Love does not delight in evil but rejoices with the truth.
It always protects, always trusts, always hopes, always
perseveres.—1 Corinthians 13

YOU KNOW I
need you

CHAPTER
one

Kat

You said you'd love me forever,
But forever was too long.
You said I was your one true love,
But the two of us were wrong.
It's deceit and lies that broke us,
And left me living in pain.
Forever was supposed to be ours,
But forever was said in vain.

IT'S NOT EVERY DAY YOU READ IN THE PAPERS about your husband going to jail. That's one way to find out, I guess.

My heels click steadily on the sidewalk as I make my way to the end of the block; just a little farther until I'm

The plastic bags from the grocery store on the corner dig into my arm, the grooves getting redder with every few steps.

It hurt after a few blocks, but I didn't care. Now I'm just numb to it. I focus on the front door to my townhouse the second it comes into view. Jail. Evan is in jail and the vise squeezed tight around my heart has been unrelenting since I read the article at the corner store.

It doesn't take long before my gaze is drawn from my building to a figure waiting for me.

Standing in front of the building with her arms crossed over her chest, is a cop. She's dressed in dark navy pants and a matching jacket that's not quite baggy enough to hide her curves. She's short, with her blond hair pulled back into a low bun and covered with a cap. My pace slows as I spot her, and I want to break down all over again.

If only I'd stayed holed up in the apartment and didn't have to eat. The thought is bitter as I walk forward. Each step hurts more and more.

I must still love Evan, because knowing he's in trouble twists me up inside.

It was the sign I was looking for, though. The one that drove the nail in the coffin of my marriage. It's really over. He's only in holding, so there's no way for me to get him out of this, but if there was, I'd bail him out and hand over divorce papers the moment we were out of the precinct.

"Mrs. Thompson," the cop says as I traipse up the stone steps.

"Hello," I respond awkwardly, not wanting to look her in the eyes as shame creeps up and makes the cold air feel even colder.

"I'm Detective Nicoli," the woman says and I nod my head, feeling the pinch from the grocery bags digging even deeper into my forearms as I shift on my feet.

"How can I help you, Detective?" I force myself to straighten my shoulders, pretending I have no idea why she's here.

"Could I come in?" she asks me as if I'd let her.

"I'd rather not," I answer, my voice a bit harsh. I struggle with the bags slightly, hearing them crinkle as I let out a low sigh. "It's been a long few days and I don't want company."

"The bags under your eyes could have told me that," she says with no sympathy in her tone.

I huff out a humorless laugh and tell her thanks, the S lingering, intending to walk right by her and into the townhouse, but then she adds, "I'm sorry for what you're going through."

With that, I hesitate.

I stand there, taking the sympathy. More than that, I need it. Tears burn my eyes as I look back at her. "What do you want?"

"It might be better for you if I could come in," she suggests, looking pointedly at the bags on my arms.

I shake my head. That's not happening.

The charge will be murder if the papers are telling the truth.

I'm not interested in hearing from anyone other than my husband. He hasn't been formally charged yet, but for it to be in the papers, there's a fifty-fifty chance they have enough to arrest him as far as I can tell, and I'll be damned if I let her inside, and … More shame consumes me at the thought of making sure I don't give them any evidence that could help convict him. As if he really did it. There's no way he did. My husband's not a murderer.

"Ask me whatever you'd like, Detective, but make it quick."

"I know you two are getting a divorce," she says and the article from two days ago flashes in my memory. "I'm sure you've heard he's going to be charged with murder, given your position in the social circles around here."

A deep inhale of the frigid fall air chills my lungs to the point that it's painful. The article was all about how Evan lost his job, his wife, and now he's about to be charged with murder. My heart thuds dully just the same it did when I first read it, as if it's lifeless.

"I wanted to know if you had any information that you'd like to give us," Detective Nicoli says and I shake my head, not trusting myself to speak.

"Look, I know this is hard, but anything at all you can give us would be appreciated."

I stare straight into her eyes and I hope she feels all the hatred in my gaze. He's not a murderer. I don't care what they think.

"I don't have anything I'd like to tell you other than that these bags are heavy."

The detective frowns. "If we have to get a warrant and search your place, it's not going to be pleasant for you." She softens her voice and adds, "I'm just trying to spare you that."

I'm not stupid and her good cop routine isn't going to work on me.

I've had to talk to cops before, years ago. I never said a word. I'm sure as hell not going to now.

"Did you know Tony Lewis?" she asks, and I shake my head. Again, not wanting to speak, but she waits for me to confirm it out loud. The pen in her hand is pressed to the pad as she stands there expectantly.

"Never met him."

"Do you know where your husband would go to acquire cocaine?"

My expression turns hard as I tell her, "My husband doesn't do coke." *Any more* almost slips out. He's done it before. He's done a lot of shit that I'm ashamed of, but that was before me. *Before us.* For a moment, I question it. Just one small moment. But then it passes as quickly as it came.

Detective Nicoli smirks and flips the page over in her notepad then says, "We'll have the warrant for a sample from him soon."

Absently my hand drifts to my stomach to where our baby is growing, as if protecting this little one will protect Evan, but I'm quick to pull it back as one of the heavier bags slips forward on my arm.

She doesn't need to know, but I want to tell her. I want to tell the whole world that the Evan I know could never do what they're saying. But I don't tell her a damn thing and I've given her enough of my time.

"Good for you," I tell her and walk past her. I shove the key into the lock and turn it, but before I can open the door, the cop leans against it and waits for me to look at her.

"Please move out of my way," I say as I seethe, my anger coming through. Anger at Evan, anger at her.

"Someone's going down for Tony Lewis's death."

"Someone should, but my husband is not a murderer," I snap. I grip the door handle tightly, feeling the intricate designs in the hard metal press against my skin. It's freezing and the lack of circulation in my arms hurts. But I can't let go. I don't trust myself.

"I have nothing more to say, so I'm going inside," I tell her, and every word comes out with conviction.

"I'll leave my card," she responds after two long seconds of her hazel eyes drilling into the side of my head. She slips a card into one of the bags dangling from my right arm.

I watch her walk away, biting back the comment on the tip of my tongue for her not to bother.

"What a bitch," I spit out the second I open the door and get inside, then let the bags fall to the floor.

My body feels like ice and my arms and shoulders are killing me. My legs are weak as I lean against the door to shut it and stare absently ahead, my gaze drifting from the empty foyer to the stairs.

I want to cry.

I want to give up.

Mostly I wish I'd been a better wife. I wish I'd kept Evan from whatever the hell he did.

I know him. He didn't do this. I don't know what he did, but he didn't kill anyone.

CHAPTER
two

Evan

EVERY SECOND THAT TICKS ON THAT FUCKING clock makes me want to break it.

I haven't felt like this since the first time I was brought into jail. It wasn't here; that place was in a small town, somewhere in the bumfuck boonies outside of Chicago. This restless need to get the fuck out and handle all the hell I created is the exact same feeling I had that first night.

Tick, the clock's minute hand moves again and I peer to my right, staring down the woman at the front desk who's processing the paperwork for my release.

My neck cracks as I stretch out my shoulders. I haven't slept a wink and I'm exhausted, but pure adrenaline is pumping through my veins, keeping me awake and fighting.

I need to get the hell out of here.

I knew something was off from the very beginning. James tried to fuck me over. It had to be him.

The only reason I can think of is because of Samantha, though, and that doesn't make sense. It's been years since we had that affair. Years for her husband to get over it. Shit, all he's been talking about for months is how he wants their divorce to be finalized.

I lean back on the metal bench as I force myself not to look at the desk sergeant, and not to look at the clock either. My eyes focus on the abstract patterns of the cheap linoleum tiles and the sounds of the police station fade into the background as my thoughts take the forefront.

The memory of that night comes back to me.

I flinch as I remember the feel of James's hand on my shoulder, showing me where the new rec room in the renovated hotel was and asking me if I needed anything else. My eyes close when I think about him handing me the key card and looking to his left and right before telling me to make sure I showed Tony a good time.

My lungs still and my vision turns red as my teeth grind against one another while my fists clench.

I can't fucking handle this. If that fucker set me up to die, he's a dead man.

Even if it wasn't him, someone laced that coke with enough fentanyl to kill. I'll be damned if I rest until I know who did it. Whether they were after me or Tony, or it was a mistake, it doesn't matter. They're dead.

"Mr. Thompson." A small voice to my right says my name and breaks my concentration. It takes every effort to raise my head and relax my body as if nothing's wrong. As if I'm not envisioning beating in some unknown man's face with my bare knuckles. I'm quick to get to my feet, eager to leave.

Each step smacks off the floor, the sound drowning out the steady ticking of the clock. My heart beats in rhythm to match my pace.

"Your belongings." A weak smile forms on her thin lips as she hands me a ziplock plastic bag and review the contents one by one, going down the list in her hands.

It's all standard procedure, I tell myself.

I shove my hands into my pockets and rock on my heels as I wait. Each second makes me more and more anxious to get out of here.

"And your keys," she says flatly then finally meets my eyes again.

"Thank you," I answer with a tight smile and grab the bag before she can change her mind. As I slip my black leather wallet into my back pocket, I wonder what James will say. Better yet, I wonder how I can get him to confess.

"Make sure you sign here." I smile as I do what I'm supposed to.

Break his jaw.

"And here," the woman adds, pointing to another line on the release forms.

Bash his knees in with a tire iron.

"You're all set, Mr. Thompson."

Put a gun to his head.

My lips tilt up as if I'm happy to be getting out of here. But my muscles are tightly wound and my stomach's churning.

All because of one question: What if it wasn't him?

No one can know about any of this shit. My heart skips a beat and I hesitate to walk out of the station. *Kat.*

My feet nearly stumble over each other at the thought of someone going after her. They wouldn't. Not when she's through with me. They can't. No one better hurt her. No one touches my wife.

I force myself to move forward. I can't go to the cops, not even to protect her. All they'll do is go after me. I don't have a shred of evidence other than a testimony that could lead them to convict me. I have nothing but my word. Inside these four walls, my word doesn't mean shit. I'm well aware of that fact.

The sky's gray as I glare through the glass doors, hating this place and what I've done. I have to tell her the truth and make sure she knows I'll keep her safe and not to trust anyone; I shake my head. I'll have to tell her I'm coming home first and with that thought, I take out my phone. Turning it on, I lean against the door waiting to see what I'm up against.

I bet she's heard I'm locked up, but maybe there's a small chance she hasn't.

As the phone comes to life, a series of pings follows the messages popping up.

A couple from Pops, the first asking where I am and if Kat forgave me. The next asking me to call him when I get out of jail. A numbness creeps over my shoulders at the feeling of disappointment that runs through me. He's too old to be dealing with my shit.

My body sags against the door, the chilly temps from the autumn night seeping through the glass.

I scroll through the messages asking all sorts of questions from people who don't really give a shit about me, and vice versa. They don't matter.

The one person who does matter, the only one I want to hear from and the only person I want to run to … hasn't sent a single text.

It takes a second for my throat to loosen enough so I can swallow that realization. I check the missed calls to make sure Kat hasn't tried to contact me, hopelessness runs through my veins before I push the glass doors open with a hard slam of my fists.

I hate that she didn't call me. That she didn't care enough to let me know she heard. If Pops has heard, she's heard.

The bitter cold air whips by my face as I move toward the corner.

I check my messages again, searching for her name like I could've missed it. One catches my eye. Samantha. I pause over her name and read her text. *We need to talk.*

My strides quicken at the thought of meeting with her. She might know something. She could be my way to get what I need from James.

I have to go to Kat first and knowing that, I text Sam back, asking when and where.

Glancing up at the next intersection and seeing the Don't Walk icon flashing, I look over my shoulder to hail a cab. I'm going home, whether Kat likes it or not.

I've kept so many secrets from her.

My head hangs low as a cab pulls up and I step out into the busy streets of New York City. The door slams shut with a loud click, dulling the city noises as I tell the driver our address. It's only after a few minutes of quiet, the rumble of the car almost lulling me to sleep, that I rub my tired eyes and think about what Kat would say. What she'd do if she knew the shit I got myself into.

She's already so close to hating me.

She's close to being over me and what we had.

I can't risk losing her, but right now either choice—to come clean, or to hide it from her—feels like I've already lost her. She needs to know, though … I have to make sure she's safe and she's protecting herself.

CHAPTER
three

Kat

"I WANT TO THANK YOU FOR MEETING ME," Jacob says in both a charming and professional tone—I'm not sure how that's possible—as my keys clink on the coffee shop table and I take a seat across from him.

It's been three days since Evan came back to the townhouse. And three days since he accused me of cheating on him and punching Jacob. That night I sent Jacob a message apologizing, but then I turned my phone off. Three days of me hiding away in our bedroom and pretending this isn't my life.

At some point, I had to come out. What a fresh hell I walked into.

"I'm so sorry," I tell him again with complete sincerity

and my eyes closed tightly as I settle down into the seat. It's a wicker chair with a dark red cushion and the smell of coffee from the café adds to the comfort. This coffee shop has a homey feel to it. Very different from my favorite spot in town, Brew Madison, but I can see why Jacob likes it.

My cheeks are practically frozen from the piercing wind whipping through the West Village, but even still, they burn. "I honestly cannot say—"

"Don't." Jacob stops me from saying more, holding up his hand and waving off my embarrassment.

I can't believe how out of hand things have gotten. As a professional, I'm mortified.

"Please, Jacob." I shake my head slightly then look up at him, staring into his eyes as I refuse to let him downplay everything, especially with a faint bruise hiding behind the five o'clock shadow along his strong jaw. "What happened the other day was ridiculous. Evan had no right to put his hands on you, and I want to thank you for not pressing charges."

"I don't blame him, Kat," Jacob says and waves off my gratitude with an ease that catches me off guard. My heartbeat quickens and it's the only thing I can hear for a brief moment while I take in his words.

"It's fine, really. I mean it, I don't blame him."

I slowly take off my coat as I tell him, "I do. I know it looked a little off." A feeling of confusion clouds my memory of what I'd planned to say.

I was going to thank him for not pressing charges.

Beg him not to hold it against the publishing agency.

And concede that I would not be his point of contact

if he did choose to go with us. Obviously, I can't represent him after what happened. I'm prepared for that.

"Evan is in the wrong in every way, and I feel awful."

"It wasn't you who did it." The comfort in his voice makes me slightly uneasy. The next words out of his mouth add to that nervousness. "I'm kinda glad he did."

"Why?" I ask quietly, the nervousness changing to something else. I should stop this. I know that much. It's a slippery slope I'm balancing on.

"You two split, right?"

"Yeah," I answer him, and it makes my throat go dry. My chest feels hollow, with nothing there but the raw emotion I'm trying to ignore. *What am I doing?* I'm feeling something other than the agony that's plagued me for weeks.

"He's not acting like it, judging by the way he talks to you. He's aggressive. He's doing what my ex did to me. And I don't like it."

"I don't know what Evan's thinking right now, but this isn't him. He isn't like this."

"Either way, I don't blame him."

I don't know what to say back. There's a tension between us that's different from what I anticipated.

"I don't like the way I saw him treat you," Jacob states with a softened voice and then raises up his hands as if expecting me to protest. "I know I only saw a small piece." He licks his lower lip and adds, "I just didn't like it. So, if he's going to take it out on me instead, I'll take it."

"It's not like that," I say, attempting to stop what he's insinuating. "Evan doesn't take anything out on me."

"It's just something about what I see between you guys. It gets to me."

"Between us?"

"How you obviously care for him, even though it's killing you," he answers with a sadness in his eyes that could rival mine.

"Either way," he continues, "I'm sorry and you don't have a reason to be, so … let's just agree to let it stay in the past?"

"I didn't anticipate you being the one apologizing today."

Jacob shrugs and it's then I get an even better look at the faint bruise on his jaw. With the rough stubble, it almost blends in, but when I catch sight of it again, I cringe.

Jacob smiles at me and a masculine chuckle makes his T-shirt tighten on his broad shoulders.

"Seriously, Kat," he tells me and moves his hand to the table, turning it so it's palm up. "Don't worry about it. I can see where he's coming from."

Jacob's gaze flickers to his white mug. I glance down at it; it's chai, and a warmth flows through me at the thought of getting myself one.

"So, we're all good?" I ask him.

He shrugs again and takes a sip from his drink. "If you're okay?" he finally answers, and *okay* is not exactly the word I'd use to describe myself right now.

"For you, miss," a woman to my right announces, startling me and catching me by surprise. The barista I barely noticed when I first walked in sets down a mug identical to Jacob's in front of me. The warming aroma of cinnamon mixed with nutmeg hits me immediately and I welcome the scent.

"Thank you," I tell her although my eyes are on Jacob.

"I thought you'd like it," he says, answering the unspoken question with a grin. "I know the shop is new, but I've had their chai almost every day and you have to try it," he tells me like we're good friends. Like we know each other well. After a moment he adds, "Great place to write."

"I can see that." I swallow, feeling a stir of something else in my chest. It pulls at my heart. *Guilt.* I feel like I'm cheating.

Evan and I are separated; I remind myself again. With all the crap Evan's done and put me through, it's over. It has to be.

So this, this little distraction ... I refuse to stop it when it makes me feel something other than the turmoil that has been plaguing me.

My hands wrap around the mug and they warm instantly as I take a good long look around the place. The brick walls and picture frames make it cozy and inviting. With the dark wooden tables and wicker furniture, I could see how a writer could make themselves comfy in a corner chair. Using both hands to lift the mug, I take a small sip and then another, much longer one, feeling the warmth flow through my cold chest. And then a third. Even though I feel less consumed with regret about the fight between Jacob and Evan, a different feeling is washing over me.

"So, what do you think?"

I have to blink away my thoughts and try to figure out

what he's referring to before a bright blush rushes to my cheeks.

"The chai," he adds comically and nods at my hands.

"It's good," I say with a half-hearted smile and then see the bruise again. "I just …" Why can't I stop apologizing and let it go?

A half-hearted smile graces his lips and it's quiet for a short moment. "Kat, I don't really like your ex."

Ex.

My heart hammers and my blood feels as if it's draining from my body, leaving me cold. "I can see why," I respond easily enough, although I can't look him in the eyes.

"Hey, I didn't mean to upset you." His tone changes to sympathetic and I hate this moment. I hate feeling weak and not knowing what to do or say.

"Please don't worry about me, Jacob." My voice is as strong as I can make it.

"First of all," he says with a gorgeous smile, "it's Jake." I can't help the small laugh that slips out at how serious he is. "And second, I'm not worrying, just being there for someone. That's all."

All my misgivings about him leave me as I look into his kind dark green, hazel eyes. He's the rugged kind of handsome I would have been drawn to back when I was single. I'm honest enough to admit I'm drawn to him now.

He's a good guy, and I can feel that in my bones.

"That's very nice of you, but I think …" I start to say and pause as I try to figure out how to word what I'm thinking without sounding pathetic. *I'm still in love with my ex, pregnant with his child, confused and feeling alone. Even if he's in jail and we're separated, I can't stop worrying about him.* Instead, all I can manage is a mix between a groan and a sigh. I conclude with a simply stated, "I'm just a mess over it all."

"Hey, let's just end it there?" he suggests. "I don't have many friends here and I put my nose where it didn't belong. I'm the one who's sorry."

"You're not in the wrong here."

"I'm not in the right either, am I?"

"What do you mean?" I ask him like I'm oblivious. I know exactly what he means.

"I—" he starts to say but then stops himself and lets out a short laugh before rubbing his eyes. "Sorry, I've been up all night working on this manuscript."

I see the opening to steer the conversation back to work and take it. To keep this relationship just business. "I could bury myself in manuscripts right now."

Jacob lets out a charming laugh and I find myself slipping into the one role I know I'm good at. "Have you thought about who you'd like to be your agent and represent you?" I almost roll my eyes at the question.

"You're shameless," he says with a wicked grin.

"I know," I answer him and smile into my cup. The smile is oddly genuine given my state just a moment ago, but Jacob has a way of making me feel calm and relaxed.

"I'm not ready to talk to any publishers. I still don't know what I want to do with this one yet."

"Want to tell me about it?"

"Well, it's about me. Sort of." He leans back and spreads his legs wider, my eyes drawn to his broad chest as he glances out the picture window at the front of the shop. "My ex, really." He runs his hand through his hair.

I nod my head and reply, "So, it's an emotional book for you. Maybe one to feed your soul, more than your family."

"I have no family to feed, so that'd be an easy one," he jokes. "But yeah. It's more just for me, I think."

"What's the plot about, if you don't mind me asking?" I pry gently as I pick up a sugar packet from the table. I have no intention of adding it to my drink, but I think best when I have something to fidget with. Again, I cling to the chance to talk about work. I'm more than grateful for this distraction. I'd rather talk books all day long than anything else.

"We were high school sweethearts who beat the odds, but we just didn't get that happily ever after, you know?"

I feel a sharp pain in my heart, one that knocks the wind out of me. Another romance story gone south. "Why didn't it work out?"

"She'd been cheating on me for a while. I found out when she got pregnant and the dates didn't add up."

"That'll do it," I say as my mind wanders back to Evan. To his infidelity before we were married but still together. And to my little secret.

"Turns out it was my best friend."

"Oh no." A pout pulls down my smile and I feel gutted for him. "Double betrayal."

"That'd make a good title," he replies and then chews on his lower lip.

A feeling of shame settles on my shoulders. Evan and I

are over, and I shouldn't feel like this is wrong. But for the first time in years, I feel *something* for someone else.

There's no way I can justify this feeling right now. Not when I haven't had time to get over Evan. Not when the thought of getting over him cripples me. What's Sue always telling Maddie, though? The best way to get over one man is to get under another. Sitting here right now, I understand the sentiment.

"You think I could sell it?" Jacob asks and holds my gaze as he lifts his cup.

"I'd have to read it first," I answer honestly, even though I know a happily ever after sells better. That doesn't mean there can't be another romance thread added in somewhere. It's not like his story is over. His eyes catch mine and it's as if he knows exactly what I was just thinking … about another romance thread.

"I'm still in the process of writing it. I think the story is going well, though," he says and every inch of my skin catches on fire. It's the way he looks at me. How his stare holds me captive and the tone of his lowered voice makes my blood race. The air crackles between us and with that, I need to get out of here. Quickly, before this conversation turns into something else.

"Send me the first few chapters?" I ask him and then reach for my purse. "Sorry, but I have to get going. I didn't think our meeting would last this long."

He half smiles at me as he says, "Okay then." He says it like he knows I'm lying, but more than that, like it amuses him.

I take out my wallet, but Jacob stops me. "Don't even think about paying."

"Are you sure?"

"You can get the next one if you really want to, but this one is on me."

I give him a tight smile, although I'm grateful. Truly I am. Even if his intentions are less than pure.

I can only nod then make my way out. It's all too much. Separation, pregnancy. Now Evan's in jail. I can't take how quickly my life is unraveling.

"Hey, Kat," Jake says from behind me as I push the door open and the bells ring. I turn to look back at him.

"It's going to be okay," he reassures me and I say thanks, although it's so softly spoken I don't think he could have possibly heard it.

I have to leave. That's the only thing on my mind because I'm so broken that the words *it's going to be okay* are my undoing.

CHAPTER
four

Evan

THE WORST SOUND IN THE WORLD TO ME IS THE muffled sobs of my wife crying.

And the worst sight I could ever imagine is her bundled in a ball on the kitchen floor, whimpering against the cabinets. Her shoulders heave as she lets out another wretched sob and it makes me feel that much worse.

I didn't know it could get any lower than this.

"Kat." Her name is a gentle murmur from my lips, nearly a plea for her to stop. She's crying so hard, lost in the sadness, that she didn't hear me come in. My voice startles her and she jumps back slightly, causing the cabinet door to rattle.

Her lips part slightly, but she doesn't say anything. Instead it appears she's holding her breath.

"What's wrong?" I ask and the second the question is uttered, I hate myself. It's obviously me. I did this. "What can I—"

"Nothing," she answers curtly, cutting me off, more embarrassment and shame present in her tone than the anger I'd anticipated. "I'm fine." She uses the sleeve of her shirt to wipe at her face, leaving her tearstained cheeks bright pink.

"You aren't fine."

"I'll *be* fine," she says, and her tone is harsher this time. "I don't want to cry in front of you," she adds with sincerity. I know the comment isn't intended to hurt me as I walk deeper into the kitchen. Kat's just being honest.

"That's what I'm here for," I tell her and then feel like an asshole. I haven't been here in days. I can see Kat's lips part with some sarcastic response, so I'm quick with my next words. "I know we're going through some shit and I'm not making things any better. But I'm here now."

She doesn't respond as she pushes her hair out of her face and visibly focuses on calming herself down. Glancing up at me only causes her expression to crumple as if she'll start crying again. She rips away her gaze and silence separates us.

I can't help but notice the curve of her shoulders and the way her breasts move as she steadies her breathing. My body is ringing with the need to touch her. The need to make her pain go away. "Whatever it is," I say, "it's going to be okay." I don't know how many nights I've told her that.

And it's always been true. "We'll get through this."

"I'm crying because of you!" she screams at me and angrily brushes away her tears.

"I'm sorry, but I promise, it's not what you think."

She only huffs in disbelief and shakes her head, refusing to look at me. My blood turns cold and I struggle to breathe, but still I walk toward her. Every step is careful and cautious. I just want to hold her. I want to fix this more than anything.

I can't lose her.

"Kat." I say her name as if it's my only prayer, but she doesn't look at me.

As I crouch down next to her, Kat stands just to get away from me and it kills me. She wipes under her eyes then turns from me, giving me nothing but her back. The cup that was on the counter clinks as she places it in the sink.

Her shoulders shudder.

All I can hear is her heavy breathing as she ignores me. Moments pass, my hands clammy and my body hot. I don't know what to say or do, but I stay. I won't leave. I can do that at the very least. So I stand there, waiting and wanting her to tell me anything. I will wait forever for her if that's what she needs.

"They broke in through the window," she states with a shaky voice, followed by a deep inhale, and my blood freezes.

"Who?"

She shrugs her shoulders, turning to look at me with an expression of disbelief and answering sarcastically, "How the fuck should I know?"

"Where?" I follow behind her as she walks into the guest bathroom in the hallway. The second the door opens, I'm hit by the arctic air coming in through the broken window. It's only a half bath and inside the sink are shards of glass.

"They didn't take anything that I can tell."

"What the fuck," I mutter beneath my breath, my hands clenching into fists at my sides. "Were you home?" I should have been here. I should have been protecting her.

She shakes her head no, her hair sweeping along her shoulders as she crosses her arms to protect her from the chill. "I called the cops as soon as I got in. I knew something was off. They went through your drawers, by the way. You may want to check and see if you had anything in there."

Fuck. My heart hammers as I stand there numb.

I don't know who it was or what they were looking for. But if she'd been here … Fear is crippling. It's the resolute tone of her next statement that forces me to move. "Are you going to fix that or should I call someone?" Her voice is flat and completely lacking in any emotion.

"I'll take care of it, but Kat, please," I beg her, forcing my legs to follow her back to the kitchen.

"I don't want to talk about it," she says without even looking at me.

"Kat, I need to know—"

"If you want to talk, then tell me how jail was. How about that?" she spits back.

"Kat, baby, please—"

"Don't 'please' me, don't touch me, don't anything me,"

she practically hisses, glaring over her shoulders as she opens a cabinet to get a clean glass then slams the door shut. Her eyes are rimmed in red, and she looks paler than usual.

She fills the glass with water and drinks down half of it with her back to me.

I want to reach out and hold her, but I've never seen her like this. Closed off and nothing but worn out and angry.

"Kat, I can explain."

"Oh, thank goodness. I was worried for a minute." Her voice drips with sarcasm, her back still to me as she turns the tap on and refills the glass.

"Please, if you don't mind, you could start with … I don't know," she says then shrugs and turns to face me, the bitterness in her voice never more apparent than now. "How about why I should give a damn about whatever excuse you have?"

My brow furrows as I take in her stance. She slams the glass down so hard I think it may shatter but it doesn't. With her arms crossed again, she waits. Her hair falls in front of her face, hiding part of her tired eyes and she doesn't bother to sweep it away.

"I don't want you to be mad …"

She reaches behind her to grip the counter, her knuckles turning white, agitation showing in every movement she has. I know right then I can't tell her what I think about James. I can't tell her that I think someone was trying to kill me or that I'm bringing more trouble to her.

I have to be the man she *wants* me to be.

I can do that. Just one last lie, once more. To protect her.

I swear it'll be the last. And only so I can hold on to her and keep her safe.

"Kat, I don't know a thing about the coke overdose or James or whatever the hell anyone's told you."

"You said you needed an alibi," Kat states evenly. She blows a few strands of hair away from her face and then folds her arms over her chest once again.

My stomach sinks as I give her just a little bit of the truth. Just enough that she'll stop questioning me. "This is why. I knew Tony was dead, but I wasn't involved." *Lie.* I can barely stand on my own two feet knowing I just lied to her.

"Why an alibi?"

"To save the company's image. We couldn't be associated with it any more than we already were." It's only a thinly veiled lie. What I've said is mostly true.

Kat nods her head, putting a finger to her lips and letting the words sink in as she stares at the floor.

"So, you gave him the coke?" she asks before lifting her head and her eyes flash to mine.

"No," I tell her and my voice is hard. *Lie. Another lie.* I'm digging my own grave deeper. I add in a truth, hoping it sounds believable enough to cover the lies. "I told you I don't do that shit."

"They're going to test you," Kat says like she doesn't believe me.

"I'll have them show you the results if and when they do," I say, and my words come out bitter.

She turns her back to me again as she fills the glass with more water. I stalk closer to her, careful not to piss her off.

"I mean it. I promise you. It was just a job and I barely drank, Kat. I quit for a reason. It didn't used to be like this and it's gotten to me."

She doesn't look at me as I come closer, close enough to touch her, but I don't.

"I did drink with clients, but that's it. I swear to you. I wouldn't touch that shit or anything like it."

She sets the clear glass down and then looks at me as she says, "Tony did." She walks past me, brushing her shoulder against mine.

"I quit for a reason," I tell her again and my tone begs her to listen. To forgive me. "I didn't do anything, and if anyone in the world would believe me, it would be you." My voice croaks on the last word and I have to swallow my plea.

"I believe you," Kat replies instantly, hating that she's causing me pain. This is why she's too good for me, but I'll be damned if I'm not going to do everything I can to keep her.

"No secrets?" she asks and there's a change in her expression.

I shake my head no, although I feel like a fucking coward. "No secrets."

"I have one," she whispers softly.

"What's that?" I ask her, sensing the air changing between us, darkening and chilling.

"I have a doctor's appointment tomorrow," she tells me

and her eyes flicker to me, right before darting to the floor. She can't look at me and that makes me more nervous than anything else.

"The doctor's? Are you all right?" I ask her, my voice low, the memories of my mother filtering in. I take one step toward her and wait for her to move back, but she doesn't.

She shrugs and stares at the countertop.

"What's going on, Kat?" I ask her, listening to my heart beat hard then harder still as she makes me wait.

Her forehead scrunches the way it does just before she cries and I chance another step closer to her. I can feel the heat from her body as she sniffles and looks away from me.

"It's okay," I whisper. I reach out to her, praying she lets me hold her, and she does. Her shoulders are stiff at first, but she gives in and I say a silent prayer, thanking God for it. Her soft curves are warm in my embrace and I'm quick to kiss the crown of her head. The smell of her shampoo and every little detail about her is comforting. This is my drug. She's my only addiction.

"Baby, it's okay," I tell her as I pull her small body snugger into my arms. I needed this. I hold her as close as I can, rocking her slightly and loving how she grips me right back.

I hold her like I have for years, and it feels so natural. So right.

"Just tell me what it is, sweetheart," I whisper in her hair as she sobs into my chest. It hurts. Every bit of her sadness shreds me. "I'm sorry," I tell her and pull back to look at her, but she just buries her face back into my chest.

It's a long moment before Kat quietly pulls away.

"I have something you should see," she says and walks off. She wraps her arms around her torso as I follow her toward the stairs.

Anxiousness suffocates me, not knowing what it is she wants to show me.

"Stay here," she tells me, looking over her shoulder as she grips the railing.

I nod and watch her walk upstairs alone. She takes slow steps the entire way. Her bare feet pad softly on the floor as she leaves me.

I wait with bated breath. My body begs me to sit, the exhaustion making me want to give in and fall onto the couch. But I remain standing.

In the silence all I can think about is the shattered window, the fact that someone broke in. If they didn't take anything, maybe they left something behind instead. Whatever it is, a picture of some shit I did, a text or a letter—I don't care what it is that's making her so damn upset. I'll fix it.

I won't let her go, and I'll destroy anyone and everyone who gets between us.

My head lifts when I hear her coming down the stairs, and my feet move of their own accord.

They don't move for long, though. The second my eyes land on the white plastic stick in her hands, my body freezes.

My mouth hangs open slightly as I glance from the pregnancy test to Kat's face.

She stops in front of me, barely looking at me and holds it out. "I'm sorry," she whispers in a cracked voice. As if this is bad. As if she's done something wrong.

"Baby, why are you sorry?" I look between her and the stick. I can't will myself to take it or to even believe it's real. "You're pregnant?" I ask her. She covers her mouth with her hand and nods.

A baby. A little life just like my Kat. Tears prick at the back of my eyes.

It's the best damn thing I could have ever asked for.

And then it hits me. *Jacob Scott.* I looked into him after that … 'meeting' we had. My breathing picks up as my blood heats. I don't have the nerve to ask her, but the words are on the tip of my tongue.

I'll kill him.

"I'm pregnant," Kat says and draws in a steadying breath, taking a few steps backward.

I almost ask her, but I can't do it. Even if the baby isn't mine, I don't care. I'll take care of both Kat and her child.

"A baby?" A swarm of emotions courses through me. "This is why you're going to the doctor's?"

"Yeah, a baby," she says and chances a look up at me. Her long, dark lashes glisten with what's left of the tears before she wipes them away.

"That's wonderful," I tell her and close the distance between us, reaching for her hands. She leans into me and I rub the pads of my thumbs against her knuckles. "Kat, why are you sorry about something so amazing? Don't be sorry; I'm so happy."

I can see her expression fall as she tries to stay strong.

"It doesn't change what's going on, but I just found out and I don't know."

"Don't know what?" A numbness creeps up the back of my legs.

"How we're going to handle all of this," she says and starts to pull away from me.

"Kat, you're mine," I tell her.

"You were just in jail hours ago and we're separated. How are you going to take care of your baby?"

"I'll be the best damn father I can be." *Thump, thump.* My heartbeat slows as what she's saying settles in.

"You said that about being a husband too and—"

"And we're going to be fine," I say, cutting her off. "Better than fine. We're having a baby."

I finally look at her stomach. I wrap one of my hands around her hip while the other splays against Kat's belly.

"I love you, and that's what matters."

"It's not the only thing that matters," she tells me back.

Her emerald eyes swirl with so much emotion, I can't stand it. "I'm telling you right now, Kat. Me loving you is the only thing that matters."

CHAPTER
five

Kat

I DON'T KNOW WHAT TO THINK OR DO.
I don't know what's right and wrong.
But I'm so aware of how I feel.
Every inch of my skin burns with need against Evan's touch. He's got a hold over me that's like a spell. It must be some kind of dark magic because he makes me forget reason. He makes me forget how angry I am at him.

I melt into him as if I was meant to be held by him from the very start.

The worst part is that I don't want him to ever let me go. Because the second he does, I'll remember. Reality will intrude, and the moment will be ruined.

One of these times, I'll let him go and never be held again. I can feel it down in my very soul.

His hot breath tickles my neck as he whispers, "I love you, Kat."

My soul quiets, the pain soothed. For the moment, I grip him just as tightly as he holds me.

My heart clenches in my chest as I swallow the lump in my throat.

"I'm so happy," he murmurs as he brushes his hand against my belly. "We're going to have a baby," he says reverently.

How can I not fall back into his arms when I know he loves me? How can I not cling to him when he talks to me like this?

I'm exhausted and wretchedly weak. Nothing feels better than this.

Every reason this is a bad idea comes to me one by one, the truth too real to ignore. I don't know if the extreme swings of my emotions are from the pregnancy, or from the craziness of Evan's life.

My nails scrape against his shirt as I push away from him. "We need to talk." I push out the words as he reluctantly watches me move away.

"If we do this, we're moving forward together?"

He nods and says, "I promise."

"I just want to be with you, Evan," I speak from the bottom of my heart and I know it's the bottom because it's all I have left.

"I promise," he says again but his eyes are glossy.

"I'm sorry I wasn't the man I should have been for you." He takes my hand and kisses my knuckles one by one before turning it over to kiss my wrist. "I'm sorry I fucked things up so badly." He doesn't meet my gaze and I can't stand the look in his eyes.

"It's okay," I tell him, desperate to take the hurt away from his expression.

"I love you, and that's what matters," he tells me again. "Don't stop loving me. Please. No matter what happens," he begs me.

"You didn't do anything," I tell him, grateful he's finally told me the truth. I get it now; it all makes sense. "Nothing will happen."

He looks me in the eye and says, "Nothing bad will ever happen to you or this baby. I swear, Kat."

"Our baby," I whisper and put his hand on my belly. He lowers his head and I swear I think he's crying, but when he looks up at me, he says, "Nothing bad will ever happen to you or our baby. I'll never put you in harm's way, Kat." He takes a deep breath.

"Just don't stop loving me," he says, almost like a plea.

"Don't stop loving me," I tell him back and he says beneath his breath, "It's all for you. I won't let anyone hurt you."

"Evan," I start to say as I reach for him, feeling the intensity of his words and the chill that comes with it. But as my lips part, a startled yelp comes out. Evan's strong arms wrap around my waist and pull me to his chest as he carries me up the steps to our bedroom.

He sets me down gently on the bed, which is so at odds with how he kisses me. It's ravenous, reckless even. Desire scorches my skin and makes my core unbearably hot.

He groans into my mouth as his hands slip between my thighs and under my panties. He runs his fingers up and down my hard clit.

"So fucking wet," he says, his eyes darkening with lust. "I love how you're always wet for me."

"Always," I say, echoing him, but my head feels dizzy and the need for him to be inside me overrides any sort of logic or reason.

I claw at his shirt, desperate to get it off and it makes him chuckle, a deep, low sound.

I want to scold him for taking so long and leaving me wanting, but the words stick in my throat as I watch him pull his shirt over his shoulders, revealing his tanned, tattooed skin and lean physique.

I lick my lips with the need to kiss him and he grants me exactly that. Bracing one forearm by my head, he leans down to kiss me, pressing his lush lips against mine and tasting me with swift strokes of his tongue as my eyes shut. He traps my bottom lip between his teeth and pulls back as he pushes his jeans down.

It's a short, sharp pain that spikes through my body, directly connected to my clit. When I open my eyes, letting the sweet gasp of longing escape, I'm lost in his gaze. Trapped by his gaze and waiting for him. I'd do anything for him. I swear there's no way I could love him more than in this moment.

"Evan, please," I say, ready to plead with him not to leave me again. Not to make me choose between a life without him or a life without shame, but he cuts me off, mistaking my plea for what my body feels and not my heart.

"Spread your legs for me." He gives me the command and my body obeys before I can even fully register his words.

Every thrust is slow and deep. The air between our lips heats until I arch my neck with a moan, feeling his thick cock push fully inside me, wanting more of me than I can give.

"Evan," I moan, saying his name reverently as my hardened nipples brush against his chest and he groans into my neck, holding himself still inside me.

"I love you," he whispers and then pulls out slowly. My body relaxes thinking he's keeping a slow pace, pulling himself nearly all the way out before pushing back in. But instead he slams himself into me all the way to the hilt and I scream out, my blunt nails digging into his muscular shoulders as pleasure races through me.

"I'll never stop loving you," he says as he pounds into me again, his hips crashing against mine.

"Evan." His name slips from between my lips as my head presses against the pillow and thrashes from side to side. It feels too intense. Way too much for so soon. My breathing picks up as my toes curl and my legs wrap around his hips.

He rocks himself against me, his rough pubic hair brushing against my throbbing clit and I writhe under him, feeling my skin prick slowly with the need for just a little more. I can hardly breathe. "Evan," I moan and again it comes out as a strangled plea.

"Kat," Evan says then nips my earlobe, sending a shudder through my body, "never forget that I would do anything for you. Everything is for you."

CHAPTER

six

Evan

IT FEELS COLDER THAN USUAL AS I MAKE MY WAY *down the sidewalk. It's empty and silent, with not a soul in sight. Not even down the alleyways or in the dark shadows. Someone's always there. Always watching and waiting.*

But not tonight.

The light snow crunches beneath my booted feet and fog fills my vision with each step I take to get home.

The streetlight outside the townhouse flickers and catches my attention.

Darkness sets in just as I walk up the stairs and open the door.

It's so quiet and my first thought is that I'm grateful she isn't crying anymore. Ever since I told her the truth, Kat hasn't been the same.

She looks at me the way I've always looked at myself. She's always sad now, with red-rimmed eyes and an expression of shame blanketing her beautiful face, and it's all because of me. I ruined her like I knew I would.

I call out to her in the townhouse. It's the same as it's always been, but there's an emptiness to it. A hollow feeling that emanates from the white walls and seeps into my bones.

"Kat!" I call out again, and my voice echoes.

My boots crunch although there's no snow.

My breathing picks up and again fog clouds my vision as I walk toward the kitchen. "Kat." I say her name, but I already know she can't hear me.

The white mist fades and suddenly I see her. Just as she was yesterday, she's balled up on the floor, but she's not crying anymore.

Crimson red has stained her clothes.

"Kat?" Her name slips from me in disbelief as tears flow freely and I run to her.

"No!" I scream as her limp body lies on the floor and her eyes stare back at me, lifeless, but still rimmed in red.

Praying for God to take it back, I cradle her, rocking her and screaming for it not to be true. A note falls and flutters to the floor with an elegance I hate in this moment. I can't let go of Kat; I grip her tighter, reading the words as the ink on the paper appears slowly. The script is feminine and delicate.

You should have let me go. You should have protected me.

It's all your fault.

And then I hear a baby scream.

My eyes shoot open with terror, a cold sweat clinging

to every inch of me. My body's stiff and hot as my heart races, pounding in my chest like a war drum. My pulse is heavy, hard, and unforgiving. *It's just a nightmare.*

"Kat," I say just beneath my breath, attempting to hide the fear before moving suddenly, shaking the bed as I put my arm around her.

It's the soft moan from her sleep that keeps me from waking her.

My heart still races in my chest as she breathes easily beside me.

As if nothing's wrong. Like nothing's happened.

My body trembles, refusing to let go of the visions. I blink away the sleep and fright as the early morning light streams into the room. The white noise of city traffic drowns out the gentle and steady sounds of Kat's breathing.

My body's heavy as I lie back in the bed, wiping the sweat from my brow and trying to forget the look on her face as I held her in my arms in the nightmare.

It's hard to swallow, the fear nearly crippling.

It's not real, I whisper. But I know with everything in me it's so much more.

Time ticks by slowly and sleep doesn't come again for me.

I didn't lie just once last night. I lied twice.

The need to be with her made me do it. The need to hold on to her love and let her feel how much I love her. I had to take away her pain. It only makes today that much harder.

There are two truths I know for certain.

1. Someone's trying to kill me and if they can't get me, they'll come for her.
2. But only if they know we're still together. Right now, no one does.

I love Kat too much.

I almost leave a note after going through my dresser drawer. There was nothing in there to take, but I made sure nothing was left behind or planted. The first thing I need to do is have a security system installed. This shit won't happen again and that's how I was going to start the note.

I wanted to write one for Kat saying goodbye and that I'll be back, then leave before she wakes.

She deserves to know why I'm leaving. Only for a little while. Only until I know she's safe.

"The doctor's appointment is at one I think," Kat says sleepily and I turn to face her slowly, my body stiff. My eyes burn from lack of sleep, but I don't care.

I welcome the pain.

"You're finally awake," I answer her and prepare myself for what I have to do.

The world thinks we've broken up. And it has to stay that way.

"You've been up long?" she asks and then yawns. There's a slight radiance to her. Her hair forms a messy halo on the pillow and a delicate simper is on her lips.

"Kat." I say her name and swallow my words.

I've been thinking about them all morning, the images

of the nightmare feeling more and more real. Every possibility of what could happen has been running on a loop in my mind.

"I have to tell you something." I stare at the dresser across the room. I look in the mirror but I can't see our reflection, only the closed door to the bedroom.

"It's only for a short time, but I have to go do something."

"What do you mean?" she asks, the sweetness she had for me vanishing far too quickly as she sits upright. She reaches out to me, her soft, small hand gripping my shoulder.

"I mean I don't think I can go to the appointment today."

Her expression falls and she visibly retreats, pulling her knees up to her chest and wrapping the comforter tightly around her.

"Why not?" she asks with a little heat in her words. With every second that passes, I can see her getting angrier. "What's more important?"

"I don't think we should be seen in public together," I tell her and swallow the painful lump in my throat. No one knows we're together or that she's pregnant. "This has to stay a secret."

"Are you serious?"

"Kat, I have to take care of some things."

"Bullshit! What about us?" she says and her voice cracks. "What about taking care of us?" She motions between us.

"I am," I tell her and my words come out strangled,

shattering the delicate balance that was here only a moment ago.

"If you walk through that door, you're not coming back." Kat's voice shakes as she speaks. Her eyes are wide and the grief I feel is reflected in them. "You can't keep doing this to me. I can't keep …" she trails off and hiccups, on the verge of tears.

"It's only for a short while," I tell her to reassure her.

"I don't understand." Kat shakes her head as if she thinks I'm crazy. As if what I'm saying is incomprehensible and maybe it is, but it's okay. The less she knows, the safer she is. That's the only thing that matters.

"I have something I need to finish."

"You need to stop this, Evan. Please. I'm ready to move forward. We have a baby coming. Our baby. We can do this, but you can't keep going backward."

God, I wish she knew.

I could try to outrun it, but not with her by my side. I'll fight it and come back to her. I just need her to have faith. I know she will. The last thought is what moves me to put space between us.

"Just believe me when I say I love you, but I can't be with you right now."

A silent sob wracks through her body. "Stop it! Stop it, Evan. Please! I don't care what it is, just leave it behind and stay with me. Please, I'm begging you."

"I'm so sorry," I tell her and hate that I'm causing her pain.

"Why are you doing this?" she whispers. "I can't believe … I can't …"

"I love you, Kat, but I can't do this right now." The words come out as if I'm ending it with her, and that's when I realize it's what I have to do.

To protect her and our baby.

"I swear to God, if you walk out of that door, Evan, it's over. I'm done playing games. You're here or you're not." Her words are restrained as she says them, each one sounding more and more painful.

My chest tightens with an unbearable sorrow as I whisper, "I'm sorry, Kat."

CHAPTER
seven

Kat

Winter happened overnight. And it's a bitter one at that.

My hands are still freezing as I stare at the fire in Jules's great room. Her home has been painted and decorated since I was here only a week or so ago. Jules didn't waste any time making the space feel cozy and warm. The soft gray walls complement the cream furniture and stone fireplace perfectly. She said it's all in "mineral tones" although many of the accent colors are a dark, luxurious purple.

"I love the color," I tell her in an attempt to cheer myself up and break the awkwardness in the room. Usually when we get together it's nothing but laughter. My face can't hide that I've been a crying mess and so laughs have been hard to come by.

"It's called Mineral Ice," Jules says agreeably from her spot on the chenille rug. Her glass of wine hasn't moved from the coffee table since I walked in. Come to think of it, neither Maddie nor Sue are drinking either.

The only one who seems normal is Maddie, and it's because she's lost her mind. I only just texted them days ago with the news I'm pregnant and she's taken it upon herself to start planning every detail of the next nine months for me. I love her and the distraction, but there's no way I can even think about a baby shower right now. It's all up to her as far as I care.

"I think the grays and yellows will be perfect for a neutral theme," Maddie says. "We could do bees or elephants and it will all match this room perfectly."

Maddie has a few bags next to her on the floor. Each from different party shops with samples of all sorts of baby shower accessories and décor. In the group text earlier she said it was a "few" things to look at. Bless her heart, she's ever the optimist. I only wish I could steal some of her positivity.

It was Maddie's idea to meet up today, and thank God they dragged me here. I'd rather be looking at tiny yellow clothespins and paper samples for invitations than hysterically crying on the floor in my bedroom. So, I suppose this is a win.

"Thank you for offering to host it, Jules," I say, pushing as much gratitude as I can into the words, but it still sounds lacking.

I'm not happy, and I just can't fake it. There's a hole in my chest and it feels like there's no way it could ever heal.

The father of my baby left me. Not just left me, but left me *again*. All I can think is that it's karma. I slept with him and kicked him out … and then he fucked me and left. This is exactly what I deserve.

I thought we were whole again last night; I felt it. Everything in me felt the love between us. And yet this morning he walked away. I must've been a horrible person in a former life.

"Okay, so menu …" Maddie says, leaning over the laptop that's on the glass coffee table and clicking the keys.

"Is it a little early to start planning all this in so much detail?"

Maddie stops fiddling with her laptop and looks up at me. "I thought maybe it would be a way to cheer you up a bit?" she says before sitting down on her butt right next to Jules. They're closer to the fire, sitting on the rug, and I'm wedged into the corner of the sofa. "If nothing else it's like window-shopping," she offers up.

"I don't think there's anything that's going to cheer me up," I answer her woefully. My hand drifts to my midsection, but there's not even a tiny bump. There's no way I'd know I was pregnant if I wasn't peeing on a stick every other day to prove that it's real.

"Do you … want to …" Maddie trails off as she struggles to suggest something else.

"Do you want to talk about what's going on?" Sue pipes up. "We can listen, you can vent. I could get a pillow and you can hit it?"

"I'm so fucked up right now …" I say and almost swallow the confession, but then I blurt it out, "that I'm actually considering starting to write letters again." I remember how I used to write to my mother when she died. It was what my therapist had suggested. "That's how low I feel," I tell them, emphasizing each word.

"You can tell us, you know?" Sue says and Jules nods in agreement. Maddie's soft gaze loses its ever-present happiness and all that's reflected in her expression is a sad smile.

"I'll probably cry too much to get it out," I respond and huff a sarcastic laugh to keep from completely losing it again. "I just wish someone could explain it. I feel crazy."

"Well, you're pregnant so you're allowed to be crazy," Maddie says as if that's a known fact and it actually makes me laugh. It's just a little bubble of one, but it's something at least.

"So let's have the complete update," Jules says and squares her shoulders as she gives me her full attention.

"It's over." The words come out easier than I thought they would. Maybe I'm just numb to them, I don't know.

"For real, for real?" Maddie asks me.

"Yeah, I'm not," I pause and shake my head then close my eyes. "I'm not doing this back and forth. I know where I want my life to go, I know what I need to do, and Evan just isn't there."

"Did you tell him you're pregnant?" Sue asks me cautiously.

"Yes." The single word nearly strangles me and I swallow down the pain that threatens me. "I told him, and he was so happy." I have to put my hand up to my mouth to keep from getting emotional again.

"I think it's okay if you cry," Sue says gently. "You're

going through so much and you can always blame it on hormones."

A soft but genuine laugh sneaks in, shutting down the overwhelming heartache.

"I told him, and he still chose to leave."

"Why?"

"He didn't say," I tell them then correct myself. "No, he said," I try to quote him although I'm not sure if it's exact, "'I have to finish something, but it's only for a short while.'"

"What the heck does that mean?" Maddie asks with her face scrunched up.

"I don't know," I say, raising my voice in exasperation and that's exactly how I feel.

"Maybe he's worried about the stress from everything he's going through getting to you?" Sue suggests and I don't mean to, but I'm well aware that I stare daggers at her. "As if leaving me is any better?" I practically snap.

Her hands fly into the air defensively as she says, "I take it back. He's such an asshole."

"Here's your tea, sweetheart." Jules sits next to me on the plush sofa, holding out a cup for me. The steam itself is comforting. The seat sinks in slowly, dipping as she gets comfortable beside me.

"I'm still so happy you're pregnant," Maddie says, offering up a distraction as she leans forward and reaches for my hand, squeezing it gently. "You're going to be the best mom," she says with such certainty even though she looks so sad.

"Do you want one of us to go with you to your next doctor's appointment?" Sue asks, but I shake my head.

"I'll be fine."

"It's not about being fine, love," Sue says. "I could take pictures or something."

"Of her hoo-ha?" Maddie jokes and Sue rolls her eyes.

"Just to have someone there," Sue says.

"I would love to go with you," Jules says.

"I rescheduled the one I missed yesterday but it's not for a few weeks," I tell them, shrugging it off like it doesn't matter. Like I'm not worried my baby can feel my pain and that every night I cry alone in our bed I'm damaging this tiny life.

Like I'm already a horrible mother and all this shit is going to hurt my baby.

"They couldn't get you in sooner?"

"I told them I wasn't free until the end of the month. I just want to get my life together," I say and take in a calming breath. "I know what I want, and I'm going to go for it whether or not Evan is beside me." Picking at nonexistent fuzz on my sweater I add, "I'm going to need some time before I can ... before I can be the kind of happy and grateful I want to be when I first see my baby ... even if it is only a little blip on a screen."

"You deserve happiness," Maddie says and the other girls nod.

"Instead of the appointment, I watched a bunch of men I don't know install a security system and fix a window."

"A window?" Maddie asks and Sue tilts her head in confusion that matches Jules's furrowed brow.

Huffing out a breath, I decide not to elaborate on

that. "I wish Evan would stop living like he's twenty-one and doing stupid things ... like leaving me."

"I can't imagine him walking away when he knows you're pregnant," Sue says although I'm not sure it was intended for me. She stares absently at the roaring fire, the crackling filling the silence that follows her words.

"I think that's what hurts the most. It was so ... When I told him, he was just so ..." I have to pause and close my eyes. I remember the way he held me and kissed me, and it kills me.

"Hey now," Sue says. "You're going to be fine regardless. He's got a situation he's dealing with."

I roll my eyes at the word "situation."

"The fact that he has any *situation* is the problem." All of my frustration flies out of my mouth. "We should have our lives together. Stability and a family."

It's silent once I've finished. Maddie looks down at the rug and Jules has an expression of sympathy, although neither says anything.

"I agree," Sue responds gently after a moment.

"It's going to be okay," Maddie speaks up although she doesn't look at me, she just picks at the rug. She shrugs and says, "Being pregnant and single is like the new trend anyway."

I let out a little laugh, and it breaks up the tension. Maddie even smiles.

"Well, at least it's fashionable then." My hand moves to my belly subconsciously and a surge of strength eases my pain.

I can do this, and I deserve happiness. I'm worthy of

that. If Evan doesn't think so, then he'll have to deal with the consequences.

"Forget him," I tell them. "If he wants to act like he's perpetually twenty-one, then he can do it alone."

I move a throw pillow to my lap and hold on to it.

"You're going to be fine regardless," Sue says, repeating her earlier sentiment.

"And we're going to throw you the best shower ever," Maddie adds, taking over the conversation again. Bringing it to happier topics.

"What theme do you want? The elephants or bees … or whatever else is in that bag?" Jules asks me as if it's all we should be talking about. I suppose it is. I'm done with Evan and this instability.

"I'll have to think about it," I answer and bury myself into the sofa. "Maybe when we know if it's a boy or a girl, then we can decide?" A light feeling seems to lift my shoulders like a weight is gone. Maybe it's the feeling you get when you're truly done with someone. When there's no way they can make it right again and you've come to accept it.

Maddie steers the conversation toward baby shower talk, and her voice is peppy as she says something about a Pinterest board.

My gaze falls on each of the girls in turn, all of them here for me. Jules catches my eye and rests her hand on my thigh, mouthing the words, "It's going to be okay."

For a short moment, maybe a second or two, I feel like it might.

Evan needs time to realize what it means to be the man I need.

Hopefully the time I need to get over him completely and stop falling for his charm is less than that. Because I can't do this again. I can't, and I won't.

Diary Entry One

Mom,

It's been a while.

I miss you guys, but you already know that. I could really use your advice now.

I know Evan loves me. I can feel it when he looks at me, but when he's not with me, I feel like he doesn't. I know I'm insecure, but he's been so weird lately. He's acting crazy and it scares me a little. You wouldn't like it.

I don't even want to tell you. I'm so ashamed.

It's that bad.

I know you never met him, but I swear he's a good guy. I know he is.

But the thing is, he's not doing good things.

The worst part is that he's not stopping.

He knows we're pregnant, and he's not stopping. It doesn't get much worse than that, does it?

I don't know what to do.

He wants me to wait for him and I love him so much.

But I'm scared, Mom.

I cry all the time. That can't be good for our little one.

I remember you crying when I was little and how you held me and sang lullabies to me. I'm trying that late at night. I hold my belly and try to sing lullabies instead of crying. I'm trying so hard, but I'm afraid I'm already failing.

I don't think I can be with someone who isn't willing to stop doing what he knows is wrong. It's not just me anymore.

But it gets worse.

I can't stop loving him. I don't know what's wrong with me, Mom. I could use your lullabies right now.

CHAPTER
eight

Evan

> *Threats can make you weak,*
> *To think of what's to come.*
> *To avoid seeing what's here and now,*
> *Living life as if you're numb.*
> *The lies are spinning webs,*
> *To trap and hold you still.*
> *The sinners hiding in plain sight,*
> *Hold your fate against your will.*

New York City is a sight that never fails to impress. It's a mix of things—the nightlife, the skyscrapers, the people themselves. But winter is when it's the most beautiful, I think.

Only the trees are wrapped with Christmas lights this

early in November, but soon everything will be covered in white and blue lights. The shop windows in Rockefeller Center will be decorated with luxe details and high-end staging, and people will come from around the world to see it.

It's stunning, but what's best about it, is the crowds. During the winter months, this block is constantly packed. That's exactly what I need right now.

I need to remove one of my gloves to turn on my phone and check the messages. My foot taps on the hard cobblestone beneath my feet as I wait on an iron bench.

The phone goes off in my hand and I stare at the message from my father.

Just a bit overworked because of my dumbass son.

Are you sure you're all right? I ask him and ignore the insult.

I'm fine.

If you went to the hospital, I text him, *it must've been bad.* On the subway here, I got the message from my father that he was being released. He said he felt light-headed in the grocery store and the manager called an ambulance. He said they were just being dramatic, but I know my father. He's stubborn and hates hospitals.

I'm fine. Go make it right with your wife, he tells me, and I have to tear my eyes away from the phone.

I'm trying.

I hesitate to tell him, but the heat flowing through my veins begs me to text my father. *She's pregnant.* I can't help it. I'm so fucking proud. Like I did something amazing for the first time in my life.

His response is immediate.

Thank God. Now she has to forgive you, right? he texts back, and I let a small chuckle escape.

I wish it were that easy. *That's not how it works, Pops.*

He messages back, *It's Pop-Pop now. I'm so happy for you two. You better make it right with her.*

My phone pings again and this time it's not my father, it's the person I've been waiting for. *I'm here.*

A few children shriek with laughter as they run by me and I lift my eyes, watching them chase each other. That's when I see her. Samantha.

I shove the phone in my pocket, stand up and put my glove back on, then shove my hands into my coat pockets as I walk toward her.

"Thank you for meeting me." Sam greets me with bright red cheeks that match the tip of her nose. Her hair's been blown around her face by the wind, even though she has on a white cable knit beanie and a matching scarf. She slips her phone into her fur-trimmed jacket and declares, "I feel like I'm being paranoid."

I don't want to be here any longer than I have to. The only reason I agreed is because I have questions as to who could have broken in and if she has a lead on anything at all. I've got nothing and no one. There's not a soul in the industry I'd trust with this information, sure as hell not with the cops on my ass for murder. "Tell me what's going on."

"James messaged me and said what happened to Tony could happen to me. He told me to lay off the demands for the divorce." Her bottom lip quivers and again she glances over her shoulder.

"As in ... an overdose?"

"I don't know." She takes a deep breath and looks to her left and right as her face crumples. "I think ... I think he was threatening to kill me."

Anger threads itself through me as the woman in front of me breaks down. "Are you all right?" She shakes her head.

"No," she says and her voice cracks. "He didn't really kill him, did he?"

"The coke was laced with enough fentanyl to kill an elephant and the cops are convinced it was intentional," I tell her.

"I would say I don't think James is capable of that," Sam murmurs with sad eyes. As she speaks, her breath turns to fog. "But he's done things before ..."

"Things like what?"

"He's choked me, thrown me against the wall. He's threatened me in the past. But he's never ..." Her eyes become glossy as she says, "I didn't think he would ever do it."

"You think he killed Tony? Do you think the threat was a real one?"

She nods her head once, a frown marring her face as she gets choked up. "He said it was for you," she speaks softly, her eyes flicking from me to the cars passing behind us. The chill of the breeze bites down to my bones as her words sink in.

It was James, and the coke was intended to kill me, not his client.

I don't give her a response in the least, hiding the

anger as my heart thuds hard in my chest at the confirmation of what I already suspected.

"What did I do?" I ask her.

"It's because of me," she says and her voice cracks.

"You didn't do this."

"You don't understand," she says, gaining more composure and wiping under her eyes as the wind whips between us and forces her hair behind her. "He wants me to give him everything in the divorce. The properties, our investments, the business, he's not budging on any of it."

"I thought it was finalized?"

She shakes her head and says, "I pushed back." Her words come out hard. "He's pushed me around for so long and he thought he could just get rid of me and throw me away like he did his first wife. But I made the company what it is today."

"So why go after me?"

"To prove a point."

"And what point is that?" I ask her.

"That he could eliminate whomever he wants."

Anger narrows my gaze as I tell her, "He missed his shot."

"He'll do it again," she says, "and I'm scared."

"It'll be all right," I tell her although I'm not sure it will be. I'm already trying to figure out how to end this. All roads lead back to James and the only thing I need to know is the fastest and safest way to put that asshole six feet in the ground.

"Please help me, Evan," she begs, and her voice is rife with agony. "I don't know where to go or what to do."

"The police," I tell her and it's the first time in my life I've ever thought of going to them. "You can tell them everything. Tell them he threatened you with that."

"He has them in his back pocket," she says bitterly then adds, "You know that. Did they tell you anything?"

I shake my head and say, "Only that the coke was laced enough to kill. It was made into a murder weapon."

"Oh, God," Samantha says then lets out a gasp and hunches forward slightly. I feel the need to put my arm out to steady her and she clings to me.

A moment passes in the wintry cold, where I think back to a few times we've gotten out of tight spaces. I thought a client here and there would go to trial, but they never did. I didn't think it was because of James, though. I thought they didn't have enough evidence.

"He'll go down for what he did," I assure her as one name and one face come to mind. Mason. Jules's husband. He's gotten off for murder, just last month. There's more corruption in this city than there are tourists. Mason knows it as much as I do and I can trust him.

He killed his father, and everyone knows it. Well, the whispers in certain circles are sure of it.

He's from a different world than me, but I know him from back in the day. Back when both of us were a little too eager to cut loose. I helped him out back then and never called in the favor I'm owed. I haven't spoken to him since I split up a fight a few months ago.

He owes me for that too. And Mason's the type of man who pays his dues.

"What are you going to do?" she asks. Samantha

scoots closer to me, almost too close, and I take a step back.

"I know a guy," I tell her and she's quick to nod, but then her face falls.

"Shit," she whispers, her eyes focused on something behind me and I whip my head around to see what she's looking at.

"It was him," she says then covers her mouth. "Shit," she repeats with tears in her eyes.

"He can't hurt you." I turn around and keep an arm behind me to protect her. My eyes search the crowd, but I don't see him.

Her hands tug at my arm, pulling me back to her. Her bright red lips glisten as she licks them and tells me, "He went down to the subway, but he saw us. I know he did. At least I think he did," she says then closes her eyes tightly and takes a step back. "It was definitely him."

"Is he following you?" Her eyes are still on the subway entrance and her body's still as she holds her breath.

"I don't know." Her bright blue gaze flickers to mine as she says, "I'm scared, Evan."

"You should go to the cops, Sam—" I start to tell her she needs to protect herself, and if she doesn't trust the cops she can always hire private security, but she cuts me off.

"It's not me. I'm not worried about me. If he thinks you know, you're not safe."

"I don't care what he thinks. Or what he thinks I know." I stare into her eyes as I tell her, "I'll kill him before he touches either one of us again."

CHAPTER
nine

Kat

H E KNOWS WHAT HE'S DOING.

Jacob Scott.

Coffee? I could use some advice. I reread the message as I sit in a booth at the back of the coffee shop we met at last time.

His place, not mine. The thought makes me huff sarcastically.

My blood rings with guilt and regret. Even as I sit here, looking from my cup of chamomile tea to the entrance of the shop as the bell hanging above the front door rings, granting entry to temptation himself.

I should tell Jacob I'm pregnant. That I'm not at all ready to think about moving on, although I wish I were after the weeks of hell and on-again, off-again hardships

Evan and I have been through. I should tell Jacob no. I should tell him sorry for not telling him sooner.

But I don't do any of that.

I give him a small wave and force my smile to stay put as he walks over to me. His shoulders shiver and I can feel the faint chill of the November air flow through the shop.

"I'm so glad you could come," Jacob says, greeting me with a smile, shrugging his jacket off his shoulders. I offer a smile in return as I see the waitress approach, carrying the cup of chai I bought for him.

"You have good timing," I tell him, biting the inside of my cheek and knowing I'm playing with fire. "Now I don't owe you."

A genuine chuckle fills the space between us as he's given his drink.

"Touché, Kat," he says, accepting it and thanking the barista.

I mouth thanks to her as she turns. She's sweet and young, but I don't miss how her gaze trails to my ring finger, then to his. She keeps her smile in place, but it doesn't reach her eyes.

My heart stutters and I wish I'd taken my wedding ring off. I wish I could solidify the separation as easily as Evan walked out on me.

"You okay?" Jake asks and grabs my attention again.

"Yeah." I force a smile to my lips. The singular word was spoken tightly, so I pick up the tea to take a sip.

I clear my throat and try to shake off the unwanted feelings. "Do you want a muffin?" I ask him absently. "Or a cookie?"

I read last night about all the foods you should and

shouldn't eat when you're pregnant. Oatmeal seems to be a winner, so the thought of having an oatmeal raisin cookie or two sounds like a win to me.

"A cookie?" Jake smirks and I almost tell him why. But I don't. I gesture to the display cases; I can't be the only one who smells all the baked goods.

"You got the drinks, let me get the snacks."

"Oatmeal raisin?" I ask him and he nods with another smirk before tapping on the table and making his way to the counter.

I stare down at my not-so-big-yet belly and feel slightly guilty. An onlooker may think I look bloated. There's zero evidence I'm pregnant at all. Other than the box of pregnancy tests. I've taken four of them now, just to make sure the pink line turns darker each time.

At least I'm not crying and wallowing in despair. I'm simply crazy with worry. My hand gently rubs my belly.

"At least I have you," I whisper in a sweet, sorrowful voice as I rest my hand on my lower belly. I want a doctor to tell me it's real. That I really do get to have a baby. This little one who will love me, and I can love them back and give them every part of me.

As I take another sip of the tea, watching Jake at the counter, I start to think that maybe it was supposed to be this way. Maybe I don't have enough in me to love both a child and my husband. God must've known it and that's why Evan left me.

I nod my head before pulling the mug back to my lips quickly to hide my face from Jake. There's a reason for everything, isn't there?

He sits down slowly, and I know he saw; I can see it in his eyes.

"Sorry," I say and shrug. "I read this manuscript earlier and it shredded me," I lie.

He hands me my cookie and I feel foolish for a moment, but then he says, "Really?"

I nod like a fool.

"You want to talk about it?" he asks, and I get the impression that I could tell him anything. I think I could tell him the truth right now and he'd know it's exactly that. I could spill my guts to him and say it's all something I read in a book. And he'd let me. He'd give me that bit of kindness.

I'm so grateful for it.

But I'm not ready.

I shake my head, my hair spilling over my shoulders as I do. "Maybe another time."

He nods, peeling back his muffin wrapper enough so he can take a bite. "Good thinking," he says after he swallows. "Very good call on the muffin."

My shoulders rock gently with another small laugh as I take a bite of my cookie, once again feeling the ease that Jake gives me.

"It's okay to not be okay, do you know that?" he asks me.

I snicker and pick at the cookie.

"You can roll your eyes and laugh, but it's true," he says as he peels at the wrapper, exposing more of the treat as he talks.

"If I'm not okay, though, that means I need to talk

about it." I point my finger at him and pick off another small piece of the cookie. "And I don't want to," I say smartly and pop the bit into my mouth.

"Nah, you can be not okay, but talk about something else instead. That's a thing, you know?"

"How's that?"

"It's okay to let something bother you, that's all I mean."

"You authors speak in code, do *you* know that?" I use his phrase right back at him.

Now he's the one who laughs. "Well, I guess what I'm saying is that I'm not really okay. I'm sort of running from my own problems. But now I'm okay, 'cause I'm here."

"Here in New York?"

"Just here," he says and gives me a small smile, but I read the real answer in his expression. *Here with you.*

"So, what are you running from?"

"Are we sharing stories?" he asks me in return.

"I'm not sure how much sharing I'm willing to do," I tell him honestly.

"You afraid you'll wind up in a book of mine?" he asks with a sly smile then adds, "One second, before you start I just want to grab my pen and paper."

He acts like he's reaching for an imaginary bag on the floor and I let out a loud laugh, then cover my mouth with both my hands as a lady looks up from her phone at me with a pissed-off expression from across the room.

Jake likes the laugh, though. Enough that he smiles widely as he settles back into his seat.

"You don't have to tell me anything. I just want you to know that you can be not okay around me. I get it. Some days I'm not the best, and it's nice to just go out and get a chai … and a muffin."

"Like today?" I ask him.

"Yeah, like today."

"I have a hard time getting a read on you, Jake," I tell him.

"What do you want to know?" he asks me.

"What do you want from me?" I ask him then immediately regret the blunt question. It's rude and risks losing him and the only distraction I really have.

"Just company, until you want more," he says with his dark green, hazel eyes staring straight into mine as they heat.

"I don't know that I'll want more, though."

"I think you lie, Kat. I think you already know you want more."

"It's only because I'm lonely." The words slip out and I hate that they're true, but a weight is lifted with my confession. I expect Jake to react negatively. Maybe to be angry or offended, but instead, he nods his head.

"Yeah, I know. I am too."

"Sometimes I do stupid, reckless things when I'm lonely."

"Well, if you ever want to be lonely together, I'm free."

I should feel guilty about how Jake makes me feel.

Wanted, appreciated, like he doesn't want to lose me.

It's foolish to entertain what's between us. But I feel so rejected. My husband doesn't want me and yet Jake does. Even if it's only because I'm the only person in the entire state who he knows.

We can be just friends.

At least I can pretend we can, for a little while. Or what did Evan call it? *A short while.*

Diary Entry Two

Hey Mom,

I have a secret to tell you. Do you remember how I told you about Markie in middle school? He's the one who was in Mrs. Schaffer's math class. He had a crush on me and passed me that note. It wasn't important really and I doubt you remember. But I had this feeling back then and I kind of have it now.

It's weird and it's mixed with all sorts of other things.

Obviously, I shouldn't see him, and I shouldn't even be considering talking to this guy, but I've been crying almost every night for so long. I started playing sad movies on the television at night, so I could blame it on that. I know I'm lying, but I'm so tired of crying.

I'm exhausted, Mom, and this guy gives me something else to think about.

It's wrong, isn't it?

I don't even have to ask you to know that it is.

I'm using this man, and I'm still married to Evan. My heart is still waiting for him, even though he's given me every reason to stay away from him for good.

Maybe I'm a bad person. Maybe I deserve all this.

I don't know. Could you tell me, please? You used to give me little signs. I know they were from you. I could use one now.

I don't know what's going to happen and I'm really tired. I'm ready for change and some sanity. The exhaustion is probably from a mix of what's going on with Evan and the pregnancy.

It's wonderful that we're having a baby, isn't it?

See how I changed subjects there? I hope that made you laugh.

I'm so grateful for this baby and I want to feel happy, Mom.

But my life isn't okay and I kind of hate myself right now.

This guy, Jake, changes that. Does that make it better?

Please tell me it does, because I want it all to be okay for the baby. Not the mess that it is.

I know it can't last, but maybe just for a little while?

CHAPTER
ten

Evan

"It's been a while," Mason says as I sit down at the booth in the back of the restaurant.

"I saw you just a few weeks ago," I point out to him.

"Not what I meant," he says, correcting me. "It's been a while since the two of us have been up to no good."

That comment pulls my lips up into an asymmetric smile and he follows suit with a wicked grin. "And how do you know that's what I'm here for?" I used to buy some good shit through Mason and vice versa. I came from the poor part of town, and he was from the rich. The only real difference that makes is which drugs you're doing. Pot or snow.

And if you want a taste of the other, all you need to

do is make friends with the right people. Long story short, that's how I met Mason and as I moved into his circle, he made a spot for me when I needed one. When he got into trouble, I got him out. It was years ago, but a pact like that never dies.

Mason shrugs at my question. "I'm going to take a guess and say that whatever you want from me, it's something I could go to jail for."

I huff a sarcastic laugh and toss my phone down on the white tablecloth, then glance around casually to make sure I don't recognize anyone. The place is mostly empty, with only a few guys at the bar and a couple in the corner of the diner.

"Are we good if that's the case?" I ask him.

"We're good," Mason answers. "I have to say, considering what's going on, I'm intrigued."

"Intrigued is a word for it, I guess."

The waitress saunters over with a beer, setting it down with a smile and I thank her, although I didn't order it.

"I got you an IPA, seasonal."

"Thanks, man," I tell him gratefully, but I don't touch the tall glass sitting right in front of me. I take off my coat and hang it over the unused chair to my left as the waitress pulls out her notepad and a pen. She's a skinny little thing, which makes her look even younger than she probably is.

"Welcome to Murray's," she says evenly. Her top's unbuttoned a little too much and the way a blush colors her cheeks as she looks at us makes what she's thinking more than obvious.

"Can I get you guys anything?" She bites down on her lip and Mason raises a brow at me.

"Not me," I tell him and lean back in my seat, not looking back at the broad and risking leading her on.

He waves her off politely. "We'll just grab the drinks from the bar," he tells her and her smile falls. She seems to falter, and she clears her throat.

"Sure, if you need anything …" she says and shrugs, "just let me know."

"So, how you been?" I ask him as the pretty little blonde walks off.

"Better now," he tells me.

"I'm sorry to hear about your father."

He readjusts in his seat, making it groan, and looks away as he takes a long swig of his beer.

"I know it's got to suck either way." I choose my words carefully. Word is Mason killed him. Shot him dead. Still, it's his father and I don't know for a fact that Mason really wanted him gone. There was tension between them and rumors they were at odds, but I don't have a firm grasp on the truth when it comes to that situation.

"Yeah," he says without looking me in the eyes. "Thanks, but let's cut the small talk. It's not often I get a call from you."

I nod and crack my knuckles one by one with my thumb as I look out the window, scanning the streets. "I think I need to hire someone," I tell him.

"You're going to need to be a little more specific than that," he replies.

"There's a guy," I say then pause and lean in closer,

resting my elbow on the table and moving my hand so that my fingers cover my mouth as I talk. Just in case someone's watching and trying to lip-read.

"He tried to kill me." I blurt out my theory. "Tony wasn't supposed to die. It was meant for me."

"You're still doing coke?" he asks as he eyes me then takes a drink from his glass.

"Not in years, but he didn't know that. It would hurt my reputation if the clients thought I was clean, you know?"

"That's what I thought. I was just asking 'cause that means whoever went for you doesn't really know you."

"I think it's my boss."

"Wouldn't he know?" he questions and for a moment a tinge of insecurity washes over me.

"He never really asked. He doesn't ask any questions so long as the clients are happy."

"All right." He tilts his head slightly and lowers his voice. "So, why does he want you dead?" Mason asks.

"It was years ago," I start to tell him and feel sick to my stomach. "I fucked his wife. Before I married Kat."

Mason's eyes assess me as if he's trying to figure out if I'm lying.

"I've never cheated on her," I say, talking louder than I should and in response to my raised voice, Mason looks to his right.

I lick my lips and calm my racing heart.

"He wants to scare her, so he went after me to prove what he could do to her. That no one's safe from him."

"But you gave Tony the blow?"

I nod my head once, the memory of his dead eyes looking through me flashing in front of me and sending a chill down my spine. "With the stuff James left in the room for me."

"So, your boss, James? You want him dead? You want to prove he did it, frame him, what do you want?"

"You have a fucking menu?" I joke with him to lessen the tension in my body.

An asymmetrical grin forms on his face.

"I don't do anything. I'm not involved in any of the process."

My body feels heavier with his words.

"Doesn't mean I don't still have connections," he adds and I nod. "So, for a friend, what is it that you want?"

"Three things," I tell him. "First, your lawyer."

"That's a given. He's already on retainer in case they take you in again."

"Second, someone to watch Kat. I need her safe."

"Is he after her?"

"He might know that I know, and I can't risk her safety." He merely nods and I add, "I can't lose her. I'll fucking lose it, man."

"The safest place for her is distance. Well, anywhere fucking away from you."

"I know … I know."

"Good thing you're separated, huh?"

"She tell Jules that?" I ask him as dread races through my blood. Before I can tell him we're not, and that there's no way I'm leaving her, he laughs at me.

"Jules tells me everything. I know the papers got it wrong."

"I'm not leaving her; I'm just protecting her. There's a difference."

"If you want the world to think you're broken up," he says, "then you need to treat her like you are."

"I don't know if I can treat her like that. She's pregnant."

"I heard." He lifts his beer in a mock cheers. "Congrats on that, man … but doesn't that make it even more important not to risk anything happening to her?"

"Don't make me feel worse than I already do." My words are bitter and my heart sinks. "How long's it going to take?" I ask him to get back to the point.

"To dig up dirt, plant evidence, figure out how to kill the guy … it could be a while."

"I don't have a while," I bite back. "Every day is a day I have to put her through this."

"There are worse things you could do."

"I can't lose her," I tell him and he nods in understanding.

"I'll watch her myself," he offers and a small sense of peace relaxes me, but only a fraction of the way.

I rub my eyes with the back of my hand and finally pick up the beer on the table.

"If anything happens to her …"

"Nothing's going to happen to her," he reassures me before asking, "What's the third thing?"

I look him in the eye and tell him, "I want him to go to jail for what he did. Whether you get real evidence or have to create some. And if that's not possible, I want James Lapour dead."

CHAPTER
eleven

Kat

"I THOUGHT YOU WERE TAKING TIME OFF?"

I didn't even hear Sue come in. I glance at the clock in the upper right of my computer screen. It's already five o'clock and time for our dinner date. The girls are taking turns keeping me occupied. It's almost like they're babysitting me and if it was anyone else, I'd hate it.

But I can never turn down a date with Suzette.

"You of all people should know that working is all I'm good for." My voice comes out flat although I meant it to be funny. God, I'm tired. I'm always tired now even though I'm finally starting to sleep like the dead.

I guess the first trimester of pregnancy will do that to you.

"Oh honey, have you not looked at your shoe collection recently?" she asks, quirking a brow. "You're good for so much more than work."

I stand up slowly, feeling every muscle stretch with a sweet ache as I do and grin at her. "Ha-ha," I say sarcastically, but the smile on my lips is genuine.

"So, what place tonight?" she asks as she turns on a lamp in the corner and settles into the one comfy chair in the room… which isn't even the desk chair.

"Order in takeout, getting pretty and hitting the town?" she suggests then takes her scarf off and looks around the office.

She doesn't even give me a chance to answer her before practically scolding me. "Why the hell haven't you decorated this room?"

I shrug as I follow her gaze. I have a bookshelf in the back, but all the books are still in boxes on the floor.

"Just not a priority," I answer her honestly. "I look at the screen more than anything anyway."

"It's like your décor inspiration was a depressing cubicle."

I snort at her response, but it makes me laugh so hard.

"Maddie should focus on redecorating in here before planning a baby shower."

I don't think the remark was meant to be taken seriously, but I actually love the idea. "I should tell her. I'd like that."

Twisting the scarf around her hand, she crosses her legs. "I'm sure she'd love to."

"Well, actually. I totally forgot to tell you, but I may

move in with Jules for a little while so Maddie could really go to town."

Cocking a brow at me, Sue leans forward with her mouth a bit more open than it should be before she says, "You sure you want to be around to hear them when they … enjoy their newlywed activities? I feel like that's the number one concern here."

I roll my eyes. "It was Mason's suggestion, so I'm sure he …" *Ugh.* The thought of them doing it in the room next to me is a thought I'd rather not picture.

"I get it," Sue says, sensing exactly what was on my mind. "You shouldn't be alone, though. Not when you have so many people who love you."

I shut down my computer and give her a tight smile. "That's basically what Jules said."

She adds, "Good. Because you're not alone, and there's no reason you should feel it right now."

Today's been so much better than the last few and Sue's sweetness threatens to change that. "Damn it, Sue, stop it," I admonish her and shake off the unwanted emotions as they creep up on me. "I'm fine."

"I know you are!" she says, pushing herself up from the seat. "And that's why we're going to go out and go somewhere fabulous."

My phone dings on the desk, indicating a text as I start to tell Sue that I don't really think I want to go out.

Holding back a yawn, I cautiously look at the message. I've had four texts today already. Each from a gossip column editor wanting a statement or my reaction to the recent events. Evan's been spotted with Samantha again and the rumor mill is churning with tales of scandal.

They can go screw themselves. I believe that was my response to each of the columnists. Probably not the best quote I've ever given. He promised he wouldn't see her. I guess I got my sign.

"You okay?" Sue asks, and I nod when I see it's a text from Henry this time.

He messages me almost every other day, which makes the fact that Evan hasn't bothered to call me back that much harder to take.

"Just Evan's dad. Wanting to drop by with some lemons."

"Lemons?" she questions.

"He said they helped Marie when she was pregnant and nauseated."

"But you aren't …" Sue trails off with a hint of confusion.

"I know!" I answer jokingly as I text Henry, *Thank you, but I'm fine. Really it's sweet of you but I'm not nauseated.* I wonder if I should ask him how Evan is. Where he is. Or anything at all.

Before I can, he answers that he wants to meet for lunch soon.

"You know, he's really sweet," I tell Sue, feeling guilty and torn about what to do.

"So, that's where his son got his charm from then?" Sue asks sarcastically then mouths she's sorry when she sees I'm not amused.

"I'll just tell him I will, but I can always bail," I reason out loud as if I need her approval.

"Yeah, that's a good way to handle it." She nods with pursed lips then looks me up and down. "You should probably put real clothes on."

"How fancy?" I ask her, setting the phone down as I realize I'm still in sweats and a baggy T-shirt.

"Let's go fancy, fancy." I hope she can see how the thought of getting prettied up makes me perk up. I could really use a night out, feeling beautiful and carefree. I'll just pretend I don't feel like falling asleep at the table.

"Fancy-pantsing it up tonight?" I ask, already feeling better than I did before she got here.

"You know it."

CHAPTER
twelve

Evan

ALL I CAN FOCUS ON ARE HIS TELLS.

You learn them fast in the line of business that led me to this moment. The sweat on his brow. The way his right foot won't stay still. His dilated pupils and quick breathing.

He's one of two things: high as a fucking kite, or going through withdrawal.

Judging by the look on this prick's face, James Lapour is fiending for his next hit.

I peek over my shoulder. His office is on the first floor. There are apartments above us and plenty of witnesses in case some shit goes down. More importantly, just outside those doors is Mason, sitting in his car and waiting for me in case I need him.

I've got two goals in coming here like this.

1.   Warn him to back the fuck off.
2.   Get any evidence I can.

Seeing as how he's in his office, goal number two will have to wait unless I can get a confession. The tape recorder in my pocket is already running.

It takes everything in me to keep my hate down, but the memory of Kat from my night terrors is all I can see. I can't sleep; I can't do anything without thinking about losing her. It's as if my sanity is steadily eroding. Blinking away the image of her, I prepare to do what I have to. For her. For us. All I want is for this to be done and over with, so I can be with her and be the man meant to stand beside her.

I walk into the office, the wooden floor beneath my oxfords creaking eerily as I do. I've been standing outside the open door watching him for a few minutes. He didn't change the locks and there's no one else here on a late Wednesday night. Just him and me. Well, not quite, there are a few broads in the far back. I can hear them from here. Maybe they're waiting for him with exactly what he needs. I wouldn't be surprised.

"Taking a break from the snow?"

"What the fuck are you doing here?" he sneers at me, ripping his red-rimmed eyes away from the computer screen. With the city lights peeking through the drawn blinds, the room is bathed in a diffuse glow. It's darker than I'd like it to be in here with only the lamp on his desk illuminating the space.

"What I really want to know is, why?" The question leaves me coldly as I stalk closer to him.

"Why what?" he asks me, leaning back in his seat and I can faintly hear him pulling out a drawer, ever so slowly.

Racking the slide on the gun in my hand, I raise it slowly. "Uh, uh, uh," I reprimand him. It's been a long fucking time since I've aimed a gun at someone. I've never wanted to pull the trigger more, though. "I wouldn't do anything stupid if I were you."

He raises his hands slowly, cocking his head and letting out a sick laugh. "So, you here to kill me now? Is that it?"

"I should, shouldn't I?"

"For what, exactly? Spit it out, you coward," he scoffs at me. His eyes appear nearly black with the lack of light.

"I'm the coward?" The ridicule comes complete with an arched brow. I have to be careful with the loaded gun. My anger is putting me on edge, the adrenaline in my veins pumping hard and every second that passes makes my body temperature go up just a little more.

One of the girls from the back room yells out, "You all right in there?" in response to my raised voice.

Before I can respond, James answers her. "Just stay where you are." Good old James, he knows how to talk to the ladies.

"What do you want, Evan?" he questions, slowly placing his hands palm down on the desk.

His arm twitches and I can tell he's fucked up.

"What's going on with you?" I ask in return. "You're not looking so good."

"You look pretty fucked yourself," he spits out without wasting a second and forces a smile to his face.

"We saw you watching," I say, offering him a small piece of the puzzle.

"Watching what?"

"At Rockefeller Center."

"Is that so?" I hate this game. This back-and-forth where no real information is given. "And what exactly was I watching?" he asks with a smirk on his face although I can see in his eyes he's curious.

I shrug and say, "Doesn't matter, does it? What I want to know is what you plan on doing."

He laughs abruptly, deeply and from his gut, but any trace of happiness is immediately replaced with pain. He nearly doubles over and I raise the gun again, my heart beating hard as I prepare for him to come up with a weapon.

He doesn't, though, and when he sees the gun aimed right between his eyes, he forces his hands to the desk again.

"You stop doing coke? I guess Tony told you it was bad for you," I say flatly, swallowing thickly as my hands sweat and the gun feels heavier.

He groans an answer I can't hear then winces again.

"What the fuck is wrong with you? You got the shakes?"

"Fuck you," he manages to get out as his eyes shut.

"You paranoid now? Worried someone's going to do to you what you tried to do to me?"

He opens his eyes slowly, the light shining from the

lamp creating shadows on his face. "The fuck are you talking about?"

"The coke you laced. You scared someone's going to do the same to you? Give you what you have coming?"

"It was from my personal stash, you prick."

I almost call him a liar, I almost tell him to shove it and put a bullet in his chest, so I can get back to Kat and end this shit. But the look on his face stops me.

He's always been a damn good liar. I know that much about him. But I'm better with tells.

He adds, "If I wanted you dead ... well, I know how to use a gun."

"You want to know what I think?"

"Sure, you can say that I'm intrigued," he retorts.

"I think you're greedy," I tell him as I lower the gun.

"Greedy?" he repeats with a crooked smile.

"I think you wanted to prove a point to your wife." I lay it out there for him. I'm not messing around; I want this prick to know that I'm fully aware of what he's doing.

"That bitch has got nothing to do with this."

There's a skip in my pulse. With a slight cock of my head I ask, "Who does then?"

His mouth parts, but then slams shut a second later. "Fuck you."

"I won't stop until I find out everything. Until every bit of dirt I can get on you is dug up and exposed."

"You know how much shit I've got on you, Thompson?" He seems to find his strength as he leans forward on his desk.

"This is a warning to stay away. From me and

Samantha." I almost bring up Kat. I almost say she's pregnant. Every ounce of my being craves to demand that my family's off-limits. But that would only give him that much more of a reason to hurt her. So I keep her name out of the conversation; I keep her safe.

I'll do anything for her. Anything and everything. Fear stirs in my blood at the thought of her being on his radar. It's gone as quickly as it came, eased by his next line of questioning.

"So, it's true then?" he asks with a snort. "You two are together?"

It takes me a moment before I realize he's talking about Samantha and referring to the rumors. "She came to me for help."

"I always knew she'd cross me. I didn't think you'd be the dick she picked to go down with her."

I raise the gun and take a step closer. "Give me one reason I shouldn't kill you right now. You and I both know you deserve it."

He shrugs. "I have the evidence that proves you lied to the cops, for one. I have evidence on both you assholes."

"A dead man can't do shit with evidence."

"The cops will find it, and you know it. You don't want them poking around in here."

"What are you doing back here, baby?" A high-pitched voice rings through the hallway and I look quickly over my shoulder. I hear the door open and James smiles.

"Oh yeah, there are two other reasons. In all the years I've known you, you've never put your hands on a woman. Well, other than Sam, I mean."

"Shut the fuck up," I say, gritting the words through my clenched teeth.

"Come on back, sweet cheeks!" he yells out. He's calling my bluff and I'm quick to lower the gun, hiding it behind my leg.

My heart beats slowly and I can see it all playing out. Killing this fucker and the two girls from the back room screaming, running. I can see the red and blue lights reflecting off the glass.

"Are you ready for us?" A young woman walks in, skinny as a rail with a sharp blond bob. It looks so perfectly straight, my guess is it's a wig.

The smell of perfume floods the room as she enters, swaying her hips and wearing light blue ripped shorts that ride up her ass.

Hookers.

"Let me just finish this conversation really quick," James tells her as the second girl walks in a bit behind the first. The blonde rounds the desk, peeking at me, but stalks toward James to perch on the corner of his desk.

"Whatever you want. I'm not in a rush."

"Hi there," a little brunette says. Her voice is softer, sweeter even, which matches her look. She's got a look that's more innocent, with clothes that actually cover her ass. She might sound sweet, but there's a devil in those baby blues of hers. Her eyes are bloodshot, and she can barely walk straight. She tries to lean against me but I take a step back, and when I do she sees my gun.

Her eyes widen, and she stumbles backward with a gasp. The two girls exchange a look while holding their breath, both on edge and realizing they shouldn't have walked back here.

"I was just on my way out," I reassure them. I tuck the gun back into the waistband of my jeans.

"I want to ask one question before you leave, Thompson," James says to my back as I turn away. "Wives aren't off-limits anymore, are they?" My blood rushes into my ears and I almost do it. I almost kill that fucker, consequences be damned.

"Ah, I see not all the rumors are true. Are they, Evan?"

"Leave her the fuck alone, James." My blood pumps hot as I stare into his beady eyes, but all he does is smile.

CHAPTER
thirteen

Kat

I T'S BEEN THREE DAYS NOW.

Evan hasn't come back or even texted. Just the thought makes my throat tight. My eyes are filled with sadness that I can't shake. A piece of me feels like it's mourning, but not ready to let go of hope.

I've texted and called, remembering how he said he loved me and this was only going to last for a short while. It was pathetic of me.

I'm lonely, emotional, pregnant. I was desperate to believe he still loved me.

The text was simple. *It's really hard without you. I'm sorry; I was wrong to give you an ultimatum. Please forgive me. I miss you and I really need you.* That's what being lonely does to me. It makes me weak and wish he'd just come back to me.

Brushing under my puffy eyes, I stare down at my phone. It's my raw heart and the very last pieces of the shattered thing that bring me down this low. I never heard anything back.

I thought it would get easier, but somehow Evan refusing to talk to me is making it harder. He doesn't return my calls, doesn't text back. Nothing. The only contact I have with him is an excerpt from the Page Six column quoting him as saying that we've split.

I remember how he said it was just for a "short while." Maybe that's how he got me. He left me with hope.

That fucking bastard.

It's like my body doesn't want to hate him and instead, the blame is falling on me.

It's my fault I pushed him away.

My fault I gave him an ultimatum.

Why am I the one hoping he'll forgive me?

Why am I the one praying he'll write me back, leaving voicemails saying he's sorry?

At least at night. And only late at night.

The days are so much easier. Although I know I'm to blame too. I know I contributed. If only I could take it back, I would.

After the unanswered texts, I started packing everything of his to place into storage. Starting with his clothes from a basket of clean laundry. Removing those clothes from my sight didn't make any bit of difference with the sadness. The harsh tears and sobs came when I started ripping the photos off the wall and throwing them into a box.

It was my breaking point, the moment I knew I'd lost it and couldn't stay here, surrounded by pieces of him.

So I moved out and into Jules's guest room.

I don't know if I'm insane, hormonal, or how the hell I'm supposed to react to all this. The only thing I really know is that I'm not the first woman to have a man leave her. I won't be the last, either. It is what it is, and every second that goes by with Evan not saying a word is one more layer added to my armor.

"What about her?" Jules questions and I lift my gaze to her, trying not to show how messed up I am. It's not her fault.

She's cuddled up on the couch, a soft cream and brown striped throw over her legs with the computer in her lap. She turns it toward me so I can check out the profile and résumé she's looking at.

Personal Assistant—Angela Kent

She has experience and an impressive résumé. My gaze scans down the lines on the screen, but it's hard for me to focus. Interviews are a must at this point; I have to hire someone to help me. Or take on less work from the agency. Both are viable options. I only need to pick one. Hopefully sooner, rather than later. I'm drowning in work, but struggling to do any of it.

"Maybe," I tell her and lean back into the sofa. I let my head fall back and wish I had one thing figured out in my life. Just one.

It seems like nothing can go right anymore.

The doubt only lasts seconds and with a deep breath, I find myself glancing back to the screen to read the applicant's résumé again.

"Hey, come on," Jules says, attempting to console me. She places the laptop on the ottoman so she can scoot forward and lean against the armrest of my chair. "It's going to be okay. No matter how dark the night gets, the sun will come up in the morning." She gives me a soft, encouraging smile to cheer me up. It's one of the lines from her first book she gave me as her agent. The memory takes me back to the high point of my life and then it crushes me.

"I'm sorry … It's just that the nights are hard."

"I get that," she says, her kind tone adding extra comfort to the small words. "Do you want me to make you some tea?"

I shake my head. "I think I just need to sleep," I answer her but I really don't know what I need, and that's the problem. There's no solution to this because it's out of my control.

"If he said he's coming back, I guess the real question is: Do you wait for him?"

"I told him it's over." I sniff and absently pick at a snag on the corner of the throw. "I told him if he walked out, I was done."

"I know what you said. But it's obviously not over, not for you."

I mutter softly, "I would be stupid to take him back."

Jules smirks at me as she says, "We've all done stupid things. Haven't we?"

She continues the conversation as she stands, letting the throw fall to the floor so she can stretch her back and adds, "Besides, forgiveness isn't stupid, and neither is love." She speaks so confidently and in a lighthearted tone as if they're so obviously true.

"Can I beat the crap out of him first?" I peek up at her with a half grin, feeling a bit upbeat just from her being with me. She's a damn good friend and I hope one day I have the chance to be as good of a friend back to her as she is to me.

"I think I'll allow it," she responds as her own smile grows.

Mason's footsteps can be heard approaching from down the hall. He's not quiet in the least and part of me wonders if he wants us to know he's coming. "Sweetheart?" he calls out and we both turn to the open doorway before he enters.

"You wanna come to bed?" he asks Jules, bracing his hands on either side of the door jamb before leaning just his upper half into the room. Like he's checking to see if he's welcome.

"I don't know," Jules answers him, but her last word is distorted by a yawn. She's never been a night owl.

"Go to bed, I'll be fine," I tell her, knowing darn well she's only staying up for my sake. I wave her off. "I'm tired too."

"It might be silly," Jules says as Mason strolls toward her and wraps his arm around her waist, "but I'm really happy you're here."

"Thanks," I reply and mean it. Such a simple admission makes my heart swell. That's how badly I need someone right now. "I'm lucky I have you," I tell her. "And I guess you too," I say to Mason, suddenly feeling awkward that he's in the mix of this chick lovefest.

"You staying up?" he asks me.

"Nah, I'm exhausted. I think I'm just going to watch something and pass out."

"I can stay up with you," Jules offers, and her voice is even peppy. She's eager to help me, but she's not the one I need.

"I'm good. Seriously," I tell her easily and for a moment I think I will be when she yields and they say good night. As their footsteps slowly quiet to nothing, the television proves useless as a distraction, because the memories of what happened only nights ago come flooding back. It all haunts me, refusing to let go.

How I opened my heart to Evan, when it was raw and damaged from his doing.

How accepted I felt when he said he was happy we were having a baby. Not just accepted, but complete and whole and like everything was going to be better than okay.

How loved I felt when he held me and kissed me.

How I didn't want to be anything other than *his* when he laid me down in bed.

I think that's the part that hurts the most. I would give up everything to just be his.

And he can't be bothered to text me back. Not even today, and I really could have used his support today. It was hard enough to keep my composure for the full two hours. I didn't say anything the entire time. But on the way back home, I felt a pair of eyes on me. It was like a prickle at the base of my neck, like a sixth sense that told me someone was following me.

I hailed a cab and texted Evan immediately. It was out of habit more than anything else.

I was probably just crazy with paranoia and all the hormones and raging emotions coming with the pregnancy. At least I'm honest with Evan, open and raw. If nothing else, I'm giving him everything I have to offer. He can't even send me a reassuring text.

Absently my hand falls to my belly. It's been doing that. Reminding me that there's another small life in the mix. I focus on taking deep breaths in and out. More than anything, I need to stay calm.

I pick up my phone, intent on texting everything.

He can ignore me all he wants, but I'm going to tell him everything I feel. I deserve that much. To at least be able to tell him what's on my mind. *I'm not the one who keeps secrets. I'm not perfect*, I text him. *I'm slowing down at work. I have to, I'm so tired. I love being pregnant, though. I love knowing we're going to have a baby.*

I'm afraid I'm hurting him by being this way. I don't know how to get better, though.

I delete the last two lines and stare at the ceiling as tears threaten to come.

I used to do this when my parents passed. I used to write to them like I did when I was a kid at camp. After they died, I'd write to them telling them how angry I was. I begged them, pleading with them to come back.

It's not fair that Evan is alive and says he wants me, when a very large piece of my heart feels like I've lost him forever.

Please, Evan. Please come back to me.

Just as I delete all the words, not sending him a single message, my phone rings. It's a number I don't recognize, and I let it ring again in my hand before answering it. "Hello?"

"Hello. This is Dr. Pierce. Is this Katerina Thompson?"

"Yes, can I help you?" The nervousness wracks through my voice at the knowledge that there's an unfamiliar doctor on the line.

"I'm so sorry to call you, but Mr. Thompson's phone has you listed as his daughter. Is that right?"

I'm confused at first, imagining that Evan's in the hospital, but then I realize it's his father, Henry, who the doctor is referring to.

"Is he in the hospital?" The question comes out hurriedly as I sit up straighter, my mind waking up from the fog it was just in. Rather than correcting the doctor and telling him I'm Henry's daughter-in-law and soon-to-be ex-daughter-in-law at that, I rush the next question out without waiting for a response to the first. "Is everything all right?"

The doctor exhales on the other end of the line, but it's not out of exhaustion or boredom. It's the type of sound that accompanies bad news. The kind of sigh that says, *I'm so sorry, I wish I didn't have to tell you.*

No. No, no, no. Denial overwhelms me.

"I would like to first apologize for having to break this news to you over the phone," the doctor says, and I'm taken back to middle school. Sitting down in the principal's office, wondering what I did. I sat there, my legs swinging nervously as he brought in the secretary, then gave me such a sad look before leaving the room. He was so sorry to tell me. They're always so sorry to tell you.

No one wants to be in the room when you learn your parents have died. No one wants to be the person to tell you. I could see it in Mrs. Carsen's eyes.

"Sorry to tell me what?" I ask with caution, but my body is already prepared for it. My heart feels both swollen and hollow, and my head light with denial. I lower myself to the floor, my hand shaking as I hold the phone to my ear.

"Mr. Thompson suffered a blood clot, and unfortunately it traveled to his lungs."

I remember the way the bell rang as I cried and the other students ran through the halls, going about their lives and not knowing my life had changed forever in that moment.

The same agonizing pain rips through me and tears fall freely as I end the call.

He can't be dead. Not Henry. I just talked to him; a voice in my head whispers the reminder.

He was the only dad I had, and I threw him away. He was supposed to be with me tonight. Like he wanted.

If I had met with him, if I hadn't blown him off ... Regret consumes me.

I can hardly breathe as the phone drops next to me and I cover my face. He didn't deserve to die. It's an odd thing to think because it means others do. But Evan's father should still be here. He wasn't supposed to go. Not yet.

My body shudders as I hold back a sob.

I've cried so many tears over the past weeks. So many shed on my pillow, in my hands, soaking into my heated skin.

These tears are different.

It's not from a fear of loss. It's not because I'm disappointed in myself. It's not even because I'm hopeless.

When you shed tears over something that's truly gone, those are the tears that never leave you. They drown your soul and take a piece of your heart. That's what death does.

I have to force myself to text Evan once I've finished speaking with the doctor. *Call me as soon as you can, please. It's urgent, Evan.* I can't help that I add, *I love you.* I'm not conflicted about adding it either, because I do.

I can't tell Evan the news over the phone, though. I want to be there for him. To hold him and ease the pain. Even more, I need him to hold me right now.

I hesitate but then add, *It's about your father.*

The phone shifts out of focus as my eyes blur and my hand shakes, but I hear it ping after only a small moment.

It's not Evan, though, it's Jake. *Hey, you want to grab coffee?*

I have to force myself not to message him. I have to force myself not to tell him that I'm not okay. With how badly I want to be held, I wish I could, but I refuse to use him.

But after an hour going by and a dozen more text messages unanswered by Evan, I cave. I have to tell him, and so I do. I tell him over a text that his father passed away and after crying for hours and seeing that he read it, I still get nothing back.

I text Jake, *I'm not okay.*

CHAPTER
fourteen

Evan

She won't wait for you forever,
There's no way she ever could.
Time changes by the day and life,
Brings both the bad and good.
It creeps into who you are,
Deep down in your soul.
The person that you left behind,
Will never again be whole.

I T'S FITTING IT WOULD SNOW TODAY. I SHUDDER AS I watch men dig the hole my father will be laid in tomorrow. The ground's hard and stubborn. Like my father, in a way. The frigid air isn't doing a damn thing to aid me in keeping my composure.

All day, all I could think is that it was James who somehow found a way to kill my pops. Mason's the only reason I didn't go back to his office and kill him. Even if he wasn't there, there's no place he could run.

I'm paranoid. I'm desperate. I'm fucking lonely.

I want my wife. I need her. A weak man would go to her and she'd be made a target. Mason assured me she's safe, and this would only help reinforce to James that Kat and I aren't together anymore and she shouldn't be on his radar in the least.

The snow crunches to my right and I turn toward the small parking lot. Mason's early. I didn't even hear him come up behind me until now.

"Thanks for coming, man," I greet him and take his outstretched hand.

"I'm so sorry," Mason tells me as he looks behind me to the gravesite. He found Kat downstairs and I'm still devastated that I wasn't there for her like he was able to be.

Every piece of me is begging to go to her. She can make me feel better—not right, but better.

"You hear anything from your guy?" I ask Mason as I turn from the two men digging my father's grave. I'm desperate for someone to blame this on. It's hard to grasp it's real, let alone just a random occurrence. I'll fucking lose it if he says yes, but that's what I'm praying for. I'm already on edge. Anger is so much easier to handle than despair. If this was because of me, I'll never forgive myself. My heart clenches as Mason stares back at me.

"It was natural causes," he says lowly with more

sorrow than I anticipated. I have to turn from him and face the nearly empty parking lot as the wind whips at my face.

I bite back the need to cry and simply nod my head.

Just a blood clot. Just bad luck. There's no one to blame or kill.

That's what hurts the most.

"I'm sorry," Mason says, offering his condolences again. He gives me the space I need as I walk off a few feet closer to the empty plot and I'm grateful for it.

"Your girl," Mason starts and then clears his throat. "You've got to do something for her." His voice is weak like he's begging me.

"You're the one who said I can't," I remind him as I turn back to face him. He told me not to. To not even think about texting her back. James is tracking my phone, just like we're tracking his. He'll know the moment I message her.

"When I asked about her being followed, you said it wasn't your guy," I add.

"This is different," Mason says like it wasn't devastating that someone could've been watching her. If they're watching her, they could be setting her up. If she really felt eyes on her, that is. There's not a hint of activity at our place and we haven't seen anything ourselves.

"She's not doing too well." My blood turns to ice as I wait for him to spit it out. *Not her.* I swallow thickly.

"This morning she said, 'everyone in her life dies,'" Mason tells me with a deep crease in his forehead. "She needs someone."

"You're the one who said she has to believe it too. That we're over with."

"I know, I know," Mason says.

"So, which is it?" I practically scream, the words ripping their way up my throat. Light-headed, freezing and desperate for this all to be over, my world spins around me, too fast for me to keep a level head.

"I'm sorry, I just … it's rough seeing her like this." I can't stand it. This is torture. Maybe it's the punishment I deserve but it's as if I'm dying from a thousand tiny cuts, and I can't stop a single one.

With a chill hammering into my bones, I finally face Mason. My voice is ragged when I ask, "Do I go to her, or not?" If it was up to me, I would. I would hold on to her and lie in bed, denying everything and hiding away with the woman I love. All I can imagine, though, is that the door would be kicked in at some point. He'd come for me, and she'd be right there.

Mason's expression falls and he runs a hand down his face before taking a half step closer. "My mistake, man, I'm sorry. Jules is there. She's not going to leave her. Just … just wait a little longer."

"How much longer?

"We don't have shit. Lapour's record is clean and there's no evidence of anything. We'll have to plant it. Including tampering with his emails and credit card data."

"How long?" I question again, not bothering to hide the irritation in my voice.

"Only days."

Days … I can wait days. Everything will be right again

after that, and I'll make it better. I nod, pacing in a short circle. Just days. The seconds tick by so slowly.

"After what happened in his office …" I voice the concern that's repeating in my head on a loop. "The way he brought her up. Like he was …"

"She's safe. I have her locked away with Jules and she doesn't even know it."

"Locked away?" I ask, stopping in my tracks.

"No one's getting into that house. And Jules knows not to take her out. If Kat wants to go somewhere," Mason says and snaps his fingers, "there's a security detail that'll be on her the second the door is opened."

"So, she's safe?" Knowing she's all right makes not being with her a little easier to swallow. She's protected and that's all that matters. I can't lose her too.

"She's safe and this helps take any heat off her," Mason answers me. "We're tracking his emails and calls, and her name hasn't been mentioned. Yours is, though."

I snort at the idea of James planning a hit on me. "And what's he saying?"

"Wants eyes on you. Wants to know what you're doing and who you're seeing."

My heart sinks at the thought. "Who I'm seeing," I echo, feeling crushed. It's like he wants me to have to stay away from her.

"Yeah," Mason says with a defeated tone. "Could mean his ex, could mean lawyers or cops …" He doesn't finish but I hear the unspoken addition, could mean Kat.

My resolve hardens, but it sends a shooting pain down my chest. I twist the wedding ring on my finger and look back at the grave. I'll be buried with this ring. Either now or years from now. Forever hers.

"Call her from a different phone, just one call?" Mason suggests as I watch the men shoveling piles of dirt. "Not with your phone. From someone else's." I barely register Mason's words.

"If I see her or talk to her," I say, my words coming out as numb as my body feels, "I don't know how I'll walk away again."

"It's a tough call," Mason says faintly.

"She's not at risk now?" I ask him again. It's fucked up, but part of me wants her to already be in the line of fire. Just so I can go to her. To hold her, and take back everything. I hate myself for thinking that for even a second. I'm weak. I need to be stronger for her.

Diary Entry One

Dear Pops,

I've seen Kat do this a few times.

Writing a letter to talk to her parents. It's how I knew back then that she wasn't doing too well. I'd give her extra attention and keep a closer eye on her whenever she took out that journal. I'm not doing too well now, and I need you. Thought I'd give this a try; I don't have anything else.

I miss you already.

If you're with Ma, tell her I miss her too. That I love her and wish you two were here.

God, I do. I need you two.

I'm sorry I wasn't there. I'm sorry I wasn't a better son.

I'm so damn sorry that the last conversation we had was about how disappointed you were in me. I promise I'm trying to do what's right. It's so hard to know, though.

It's too many lies to know what the truth is. Too many secrets to hold on to what's real.

I'm afraid of losing everything. It's like it's all crumbling around me and I can't stop it.

I'm so damn alone, and it's my fault. I'm terrified to be close to anyone right now.

I need you to do me a favor. You gotta look out for Kat.

She misses you and she's not okay.

She used to say that when she'd write, her parents would be there in some way. She said she knew they were watching. She knew they heard. I hope you can hear me now.

Can you go to her? Please?

Give her a sign that you're there and that you love her.

I'm trying, Pops, but it's so hard to know if I'm doing the right thing.

If I lose her too, it's over for me. There's nothing left.

So please, don't watch over me. Stay with her.

I love you forever.

CHAPTER
fifteen

Kat

It's memories that hold me back,
The visions of yesterday.
Back when we were so happy,
And our faith did not yet stray.

"**T**HANKS FOR MEETING ME HERE."

"No problem," Jake responds with a charming smile as he sits down across from me in the booth.

We're back at Brew Madison and not the café closer to Jake's place. It's "my place," but it feels different. Everything feels a bit different now. Nothing feels like it did once; that feeling of being home isn't the same without Evan.

"Tired of the chai?" he asks, and I have to laugh.

"No, it's just that Jules, my friend who I'm staying with for a bit, wanted to meet across the street after we're done, so I asked her driver to bring me here."

"Ah, gotcha. What are you guys going to do?" His question is casual as he looks up at the menu across the wall. It's a large black chalkboard with all their drinks written in elegant flowing script. I'm pretty sure it's not actually handwritten, but I could be wrong.

"The chai is better at your place," I tell him and snag my caffeine-free pumpkin spice coffee from off the small table. Apparently, Maddie's tastes have rubbed off on me. Either that or the baby has ruined my taste buds and given me a temporary sweet tooth.

He chuckles as I take a large gulp then tell him, "I think we're getting dinner at a little Italian place Jules loves. Or maybe heading to the new bar below the hotel a few blocks over." I shrug and add, "She hasn't decided yet, but it's girls' night, so we're doing something."

He lays his coat over the back of his seat as he stands. "I'm going to go with straight black coffee."

"Oh?" I ask him. "Is it one of those days?"

"You tell me," he responds and instantly my smile falls. It's been a week since Henry died and each day is worse than "one of those days." They blur together and time has flown by, but somehow, it's only been a week.

"Give me a sec?" he asks me before leaving, as if he's checking on my well-being, gripping the back of the chair. I nod, not trusting myself to speak.

My fingers play at the edge of my coffee cup. I wore lipstick today and the outline of my lips mars the white rim.

There's a statistic I read once about how lipstick sales and alcohol sales both go up during depressions, while sales for everything else plummet.

The alcohol … well, you drink when you're happy and you drink when you're sad.

The lipstick is because in hard times, we just want to feel special, pretty. We want to feel like we're worth it. As in, if we look pretty and put together, then maybe we can be.

I need to buy more lipstick, I think.

It only takes a moment of me checking my phone before he's back with a brighter spirit and the robust smell of fresh black coffee joining him from the cup in his hand. "So, what's going on?"

"Wow, that was fast," I say to stall a moment longer.

"I'd rate them an A-plus for the service. I'll have to admit that," he answers with a pleasant smile.

I give him a soft one in return, but I can feel it breaking down as I try to formulate an answer to his question.

"Evan's father died." The truth rushes out and my expression crumples regardless of how hard I'm trying to keep it in place.

"Shit," Jake murmurs beneath his breath as I desperately work to maintain my composure. "You all right?"

"I'm fine," I answer in a choked voice, refusing to cry again. "I'm dealing with it. It's not the first time I've lost a family member, but it still hurts."

"What happened?"

"It was sudden. He had a blood clot that traveled to his lungs." As I pick up a napkin from the table and blot under my eyes, I remember the doctor's voice and how calmly he spoke. My lashes graze the napkin as I blink and it comes back black.

"I'm sorry; I'm such a mess," I tell him, flipping the napkin to the other side and being careful not to smudge my makeup too much.

"Don't be." It's only then that I realize how close he is. He's so warm. "Evan," I say, blurting out his name as my tired eyes feel heavy and the need to be held makes my body hot. My fingers itch to lay across Jake's lap. "I tried to call him and got his voicemail."

"About his father?" Jake asks, and I find myself leaning closer to him. Jake doesn't let on that there's any more tension between us than usual. The air between us has shifted. It's something closer and vulnerable. Something I should be wary of, but I need it. God, I need it.

I nod once, twisting the little shreds of the napkin I'm destroying in my lap. "The doctor called me. I was my father-in-law's emergency contact." My throat tightens yet again and my words are choked, thinking about how I was listed as his daughter in Henry's phone.

"And Evan?"

"He didn't answer."

Jake leans back, putting a bit of distance between us and seems to question whether or not he wants to respond. He takes a heavy breath as if he's going to, but sips his coffee instead. I study his face as he stares straight ahead.

"I'm sorry, I shouldn't even be talking about this. I just—"

"Stop saying you're sorry, Kat." Jake turns his head and

gazes deep into my eyes as he tells me, "You have nothing to be sorry for, and I don't understand why anyone would make you feel like you do."

My breath comes in shorter bursts, my heart beating faster. But all I can think about is how I wish Evan would say those words to me.

My teeth sink into my bottom lip as I reply, "I am sorry, though." I don't know what else to say. It's just how I feel.

"Well, I'm sorry too. I'm sorry about your father-in-law. And I'm sorry your ex isn't there for you. I'm sure he's going through his own things, but it doesn't seem right that he's ignoring you like that. He's got to know it hurts you."

"He doesn't feel like my ex most of the time," I admit to Jake with my eyes focused on my fingers as I continue to shred the napkin.

I'm anxious for Jake's response. It would lift a weight and burden for someone to understand, and I feel like Jake can. Even if he can't, I don't think he'll judge me. I hope he won't.

"You've been married for years, right?" I nod at his question. "And you only just split?" I nod again to confirm.

"You're going through a lot, and he's not even talking to you. I don't get this guy. I wouldn't throw you away like that."

"I don't think he's throwing me away so much as putting me to the side while he tries to ..." An uneasy sigh slips into the silence when I can't finish my own thought.

"I read in the papers about what he's got going on," Jake says, and I'm forced to look at him, my heart beating slowly as I wait for his judgment. "I don't get how the two of you fit together, honestly."

"We have more in common than you'd think."

"Still have? Or had?" he asks me. Without waiting for a reply, he shakes his head. "Tell me to fuck off if you want," he offers then closes his eyes and takes a quick sip of coffee. "I'm only here if you want to talk. And if I cross a line—"

"You're not crossing any line," I reassure him and find myself reaching out, letting my hand fall on top of his. Mostly for fear of him backing away and leaving me with nothing again. "I don't talk to anyone else really." The plea is unsaid, but Jake hears it. I'm already a burden to my friends. I know I am, even if that's what friends are for. The one thing I know, though, is that they'll remember everything Evan's done, and they'll hate him like I do right now for treating me how he has. Even if they don't say it. So all of this animosity and worry over him and his actions? I can't give it to them. I need someone else. Someone like Jake.

His soothing gaze assesses me and stays on mine as he tells me, "I don't want you to get upset with me because of an opinion I have when I only know a small fraction of the truth. I know the past goes deeper than that."

It's small kindnesses that kill the pain. The tiny bits break down walls, making them crumble all because they hit at just the right spot, at just the right time.

"Just don't hate me for still loving him," I whisper.

"I think you still have feelings for him because you haven't let anyone else in," he says and leans just a bit closer to me.

If Evan would give me just a little, I wouldn't be here. The thought flies through my mind as Jake leans forward a bit more, his gorgeous dark green, hazel eyes focused on my lips.

If Evan would only comfort me or let me comfort him, I wouldn't have even called Jake, I think as I close my eyes and breathe in the masculine scent of Jake's cologne. The deep forest fragrance fills my lungs as he gently presses his lips against mine.

If Evan really wanted me, if he cared about me ... the thought is lost when my hands move to Jake's hair, my fingers spearing through it as my lips part and Jake deepens the kiss.

The problem is that when my eyes are closed, I picture Evan. It's his fingers that thread through my hair and cup the back of my head. It's his lips pressed against mine.

The problem is when I open my eyes, it's not Evan. No matter how much I want it to be him.

Diary Entry Three

Dear Mom,

I really could use you today. You had such great advice when I was younger.

Evan's father passed away and I don't know what to do. I want to be there for him because I love him even though he's not here for me. But he didn't want me to be there for him. Not even at the funeral. He hardly looked at me.

Mom, I think he blames me in some way. Or there's something I don't know. I don't understand it. You know how you told me to be honest with my emotions? I feel like

I'm dying inside. I can't describe how badly it feels to stand near him and be completely ignored because "hurt" doesn't do it justice. It's an emptiness I don't know how to fill.

I love him so much, but I cried alone in the car at the funeral. He didn't hold me. He didn't talk to me. He only hugged me like he hugged everyone else. Like I was no one special.

I thought for a second he would let me cry in his arms. Or that he would cry in my arms like he did when his mom died. But he didn't. He just left.

He didn't need me, Mom. He didn't need me at all and it feels like I need him just to breathe.

There's something else too. Something that you might not like. Or I don't know, maybe you'll like it now that you know what Evan did.

I kissed someone else.

I can't help feeling like I'm cheating on Evan.

But if Evan doesn't want me, it's okay, right? It doesn't feel okay. Separated or divorced, I still love Evan.

This guy, his name's Jake, he treats me like he cares about me. Not that we've done anything really. I don't even know him. I think I want to, though, and that scares me.

My heart belongs to Evan, but there's someone else who wants to take it.

Seeing Evan at the funeral is what broke me.

I don't know what to do.

I tell you that a lot, don't I? That I don't know what to do. But for the first time, I want to do something. I'm ready for something to change. I know you'd know what to do.

I wish you were here. I miss you. I love you.

CHAPTER
sixteen

Evan

THE PILES OF DIRT ARE GROWING LARGER. THE metal shovels pierce the frozen soil. The sound cuts through my bones, one and then another and another.

It's been constant as I stand here helplessly. I've never been colder, the bitter wind and blustery snow besieging my body, but I still don't move.

I can't take my eyes from the two graves.

The shovels spill the dirt, the piles mounting as my eyes drift to the tombstones.

The first my father, a man who died before his time. A death of tragedy.

And then to my wife's. My love's. No one believes me. He put her there. James killed her.

My eyes pop open wide when I hear Kat whisper, "It's all your fault."

I wake up gasping for air, my heart pounding and I swear I can feel Kat's hot breath on my neck even though I'm alone. My eyes dart around the room as I slowly lift my body into a sitting position on the bed.

Just a terror. The same as last night.

I'm quick to grab the video monitor for the security system from the nightstand and flick the button on to bring it to life. Mason set it up for me to keep a close eye on her.

It's only when I see Kat in bed that my heart starts to calm, and my heated skin seems to succumb to the chill of reality.

She's okay.

I close my eyes and when I open them, the monitor displays an image of her rolling over in bed. *To my side.* My fingers brush the glass where she is. I'll be there soon. I'll be with her and it'll all be over.

It's that promise to myself that brings me any sleep at all anymore. *It'll be over soon and then I'll be with her.*

"There's a lot of shit you aren't going to like," Mason states matter-of-factly the second I close the door to his car. He doesn't even wait for my ass to hit the seat. He's situated outside the park and I focus on the people walking by. Moving through their day and carrying on with their lives, while mine's slowly deteriorating into nothing.

I needed this meetup to get the fuck out of this rut

and talk to someone. Even if it means hearing something I'm not going to like.

"Let's start with the easiest."

"You have a tail. Hired by Lapour," he says, and his sentences are short, clipped. I nod my head. I figured as much. I've been scoping James out and James is doing the same in return.

"The cops are coming around your place more often too and they've been poking around your family home, looking through the garbage. A few tags on the station's search engine too."

"They're not going to give up, are they?" It's not really a question. The leather of the seat groans as I lay my head back.

"They just need one thing to pin it on you."

"James has the evidence they'd need to do it." The photos come to mind and anxiousness makes my chest tighten. I'm waking up to heart palpitations and I'm constantly exhausted, but not able to sleep. My right leg rocks from side to side as Mason speaks.

"We can wipe them from his computer, but the hard copies will have to wait until tomorrow. My associate will ensure the place is clean, but then he'll know."

"That works. Whatever it costs."

"It takes time to get a batch of drugs that matches," Mason says and I know it's not about the money. It's about the time and executing it correctly.

"It would have been easier if we'd found it on him," I say, stating the obvious.

"Yeah, it would have," he agrees and then it's quiet.

"I'm failing. All this money paying other people to do shit and we're coming up empty."

"You're doing everything you can."

I can't stand the waiting anymore. "I want this over with," I confide in him. A couple of days turned into a week. And now the weeks are bleeding into one another.

"I'm walking around this city," I tell him, "stalking a man who should be dead. I *need* to do something." It's killing me to wait, driving me fucking crazy. I can practically feel my sanity slipping away.

"You have to be careful when you … take care of someone," he says as if I'm being impatient. "If you're reckless, you get caught.

"Besides, I don't have anything on James. Not a shred of evidence that shows he purchased the fentanyl."

"We need evidence or to set him up if there isn't any. Or we can just murder him and end it all." The thought has been festering in the back of my skull. Picking away at me. I just want to kill the fucker and be done with this.

"You kill him before it's ready, and the cops will be looking for his murderer. Is that what you want?"

I know he's right, and I can't answer. I respond with the only thing that matters. "I need my wife back."

"That's the other thing," he tells me while looking out his window.

"What thing?" I question, a deep groove settling down the center of my brow as I stare at the back of his head, willing him to look at me. "About my wife?"

"She's seeing someone," he answers and it's like white noise.

"You're wrong." Time slows. She isn't. There's no way she's seeing someone.

"She went out yesterday and we kept an eye on her like I promised you we would. My guys saw some things."

That's when a man's face comes back to me. My hands clench into tight fists at my side as I shake my head. Jacob whatever the fuck his last name is. My breathing comes in ragged pants as he says, "Jacob Scott is his name. A potential client of hers."

"Not my wife," I say, biting out the words although I already know it's true. "She's not going to move on so fast."

The worst part is that I don't even blame her. I'm dying inside. Every night I think about how my father should still be here and my wife should be in bed with me. Instead I'm alone, clutching a fucking T-shirt Pops always wore. He gave it to me when he gained a little weight and it didn't fit him any longer. It's just a shirt from a shop he used to work at. The shop's not around anymore.

I didn't give a shit about it back then, it was just a shirt, but all I can see when I hold it now is him. It's funny how the little things that don't matter are the most sentimental when you lose the ones you love.

That's my life. Hiding away and mourning my father alone. Hating myself and not being able to fix it all. I can't fix a damn thing.

"I told you she wasn't doing well," Mason says like I should have known better.

My teeth grind against each other as I seethe. "I can't do both at the same time, lead her on that we're broken up, but also be there for her." Pounding my fist against the window once like a madman, I hold on to the anger. I'll prolong every other emotion I can until I'm forced to deal with it at night when sleep refuses to comfort me. I know I must look like I'm fucking unhinged, but I am. So, I suppose it's fitting. "I can't protect her and have her in my life at the same time. There's no way for me to do it!" Exasperation gets the better of me.

"Well, if you're not there for her, someone else will be."

My heart's in my throat. That's the only explanation for what I feel. It's not in my chest where it's supposed to be. Only pain lingers there.

"I want to kill him. That Jacob fuck."

"Now I know that one isn't serious."

"He's seeing my wife!" I bite down on the inside of my cheek to keep from screaming, but Mason doesn't react.

He's silent as my rage slowly subsides.

"What would you do?" I ask him out of desperation as I imagine her calling him. Alone and desperate for someone to take away her pain.

Mason answers with a shrug, "Kill the asshole."

"You're a real wiseass, you know that?"

"It could be worse," he says.

"How's that?"

"She cried for a while when she got back from dinner with Jules."

I wait for him to continue, not understanding. "Why was she crying?"

"After seeing the guy, she cried all night. She's not moving on. She's not okay, Evan."

"What am I supposed to do? She's everything to me. And all I can see, all I dream about at night is her dying because of me." Mason doesn't answer me.

No one has an answer for me. "If I lose her, I have nothing. There's no reason to live if I don't have her."

"You could always go with the locking her in a room option. She likes her office, right?" Mason jokes and I don't know whether to thank him for lightening the mood, or punch his fucking face in.

"Do you think James would go after her if I took her back?" I ask him. "Tell me honestly."

"If someone wanted to hurt you, the first thing they'd do is go after her." Mason says exactly what I already knew, and I rest my head against the window.

"He still might, but the chance of that seems low. Right now, James is only interested in three people: you, Samantha, and a man named Andrew Jones. Obviously, a cover."

Before I can ask, Mason adds, "We're paying him a visit soon. As soon as we track down his location."

I nod, agreeing with the plan, but all I can think about is that prick with his hands on my wife.

"What if we paid Jacob a visit?"

"You really think that's the way to go? Like Kat won't find out?" he asks me, and I grit my teeth.

"What if she goes home? What if you go home? Just be quiet about it. Rent a hotel room and make sure you're seen there for your tail. But go to her at night and make sure she keeps quiet."

"Kat can't keep a secret for shit."

"She's talking about going back home anyway. You're going to need to be there."

"You think she'd be okay with me just slipping in at night? Maybe if I told her what's going on. But in and out, coming and going as I please? She'd kill me."

"Don't tell her shit. Are you fucking crazy?"

"Lie to her? Kat's always been able to see right through me. Lying is what made all this worse."

"I'm not saying lie to her. I'm just saying this is how it has to be. Right now, she needs comfort … She'll take what you can give her. James thinks you're with Samantha, so be seen with her, then head over to your place."

The very idea of being seen with Samantha makes my stomach coil. "You want my wife to hate me?"

"It's the only real option you have right now," he says and looks me in the eyes to add, "She'll never know."

He's a fool to think that. She'll find out. There's no fucking way I'm going to do that to her. She deserves better than that.

CHAPTER
seventeen

Kat

I HAVE TO TELL EVAN ABOUT JAKE, BUT HE DOESN'T want to talk to me.

He's ignoring me. Intentionally hurting me.

Yet there's still a sense of obligation. As if I owe it to him to let him know that I'm moving on now. I've finally got a grip on my self-respect, but I need him to know it. I roll my eyes at the thought and heave out an aggravated sigh.

I don't care if it's weak or pathetic. He was everything to me.

I nearly trip as I realize what I thought. *Was.*

Is it really over? I struggle to breathe in the cold air as I think maybe a small part of me wants to move on. No, that's not it. It's simply accepting that it's time to move on.

Say something, I'm giving up on you … song lyrics play through my head as my throat dries and I force myself to keep walking up the sidewalk to 82 Brookside. Evan's family home.

The sad lyrics of the soft song are what keep me from knocking on his door at first. I attempt to compose myself because if Evan doesn't open this door, or worse, he does but doesn't hear me out? Then I have no hope left.

I know deep down in my gut, this is my last and final effort.

Say something, I'm giving up on you … and then the melody stops, a feminine voice cutting through. The voice of a woman I recognize. Sadness freezes over, replaced quickly by something … more gruesome.

Samantha.

I hear her laugh and then a muted voice. His voice. She's in there with him. Shock keeps me paralyzed. I listen a moment longer, denying it at first.

The only movement I can make is to hide my hands in my coat pockets as the winter wind brutalizes me. I thought my heart was already broken. Apparently, it was only torn because at this moment, there's no denying my heart's been ripped ruthlessly in half.

I'm numb as I stand in the harsh cold, trying to listen to the faint sounds as I lean my body toward the window to my right. I can barely see her, and I can't see him at all.

There's no way I can make out what they're saying, but I watch her put on her coat.

It's funny how anger can so easily replace sadness. Almost like rock paper scissors. Anger beats sadness, sadness beats … I don't know what, and in this moment, I don't care in the least.

My heartbeat rages; my breathing shallows as I watch that woman I once trusted standing in Evan's parents' home. He can't really be with her.

Time passes, maybe a minute more before I come to terms with it.

What a fucking fool I was.

This is why he left me. Of course. My breathing falters as I take a few steps back from the door, my warm breath turning to fog in front of me. Shoving my hair out of my face, I collect myself before I can fully fall apart.

With my arms wrapped tight around my shoulders, I hug myself as I walk aimlessly down the street. My shoes crunch the thin layer of fallen snow beneath my feet as I get farther and farther away. I let my mind whirl and my emotions stir into a concoction of self-doubt and recklessness.

"He thought I would wait for him while he had one last fling?" I whisper under my breath but then shake my head. "Maybe he's trying to pick which one of us he wants . . ."

Like a madwoman I talk to myself, ignoring the horns honking and cars speeding along the street next to me. I let out a sarcastic laugh and think, *his choice is made.*

He already left me, and I already told him it was over.

How dumb can I really be?

My hands fumble inside of my jacket as I turn the street corner. I bite down on the fabric of my glove and pull it off so I can unlock my phone.

Evan's cheating on me. I tell Jules first. I've talked to her more than anyone else since she's welcomed me into her house.

No, he can't be! She's quick to respond and I find myself standing still in the middle of the busy sidewalk, texting her back. Everyone walks around me, ignoring me and my mental breakdown.

I'm pregnant with his child and he's cheating on me.

Why would you think that? she texts back as I type my response.

I just saw her.

Saw who? she asks.

Samantha.

And they were kissing??? That bastard!!

I bite the inside of my cheek and hate that I can't say yes. They weren't kissing. I told him to stay away from her and she's inside his house, though. Isn't that enough?

I didn't see them kiss. She's in his house.

What were they doing? she asks, and I find my anger turning on her.

I don't know!

What were you doing, spying??

OMG Jules! YES, of course, I was! I stand there numb, reading the text messages and feeling like I truly am crazy.

What did he say?

About them? I didn't go in, I text her. I'm left with silence for a moment with no response back. The wind seems to pick up and my ears burn from the cold. Or maybe from people talking about me.

I'm going to get proof. I text Jules and spin around on my heels, shoving the phone into my coat pocket and ignoring the dings of her return messages.

I'll confront that bastard and make him pay for the

hell he's put me through. All the while I work myself up. Each step back to his house is taken with stronger and stronger resolution.

Until I get there and his car is gone, and just like my gut told me the second I saw the empty spot in front of his house, the door is locked.

"Motherfucker," I scream out as I bang my fists against the door. The chill in the air makes each impact hurt more and more.

I start to text him even though my hands are aching from the freezing cold. One line saying, *I know.* And then I backspace until it's erased. That's not good enough, it's too mysterious. I text him a paragraph about what I saw, but I delete that too, knowing he'll just deny it.

Outside of his parents' house, outside of the house where I fell in love with him, the light dims from the sinking sun and the sudden sheets of gray signal more snow is coming.

Defeated, I slip my phone in my pocket, realizing only now that I've been trembling.

I'm not going to text him or confront him. Nothing. I'll figure out the truth and make sure I have evidence, but I'm giving Evan exactly what he gave me … nothing.

Diary Entry Four

Mom,

I'm worried about the things that I think sometimes.

I'm worried about how angry I get. Did you get like that ever?

I don't know if you would have. I did it to myself by marrying Evan.

I'm filled with anger more than anything anymore. I don't want to be like this, but it's what he's done to me. Maybe that's an excuse. That's probably what you'd tell me, isn't it? I'm responsible for my own actions and no one else's.

I've never been this angry, and I'm afraid of what I'm going to do.

CHAPTER
eighteen

Evan

I HAVEN'T BEEN THIS NERVOUS SINCE KAT AND I went out on our first date.

It was an easy date, a place I knew well. *My club.* I didn't own it; I never got into commercial real estate, although I have thought about it. It was still my club, though. At least that's how I felt. I should've felt in control and powerful to meet her in front of the doors, the music drifting out into the street, but one look at her stepping out of her car had my heart pumping faster and the back of my neck sweating.

Kat's always been able to stun me like that.

As if I don't already know she's beautiful.

It's something else, though, that's got me this nervous.

It's the sense that I can't hold on to her no matter what

I do. That's the feeling I had flowing through my veins that night, and that's the feeling flowing through me now as I get ready to step up to the doors of Mason's house in the Berkshires.

I check my phone again to see if I have any more texts from him, but I don't. The last one said she was packing her stuff and planning on moving back to the townhouse.

I rap my knuckles on the hard oak doors, the cold air making it hurt just a bit. My body urges me to do it harder, to embrace the pain and focus on that and not the anxiety of rejection.

I would deserve it, after all.

The door opens in one tug, and the glow from the foyer chandelier carries to the porch. There she is. Holding the door open with her lips parted in shock.

"Evan." She says my name as she stands perfectly still.

A faint dusting of snow settles around me as I take her in. From the white socks on her feet, to the silk pajamas that must be a gift from Jules, because I've never seen them before in my life.

"Hey," I greet her and then swallow the lump in my throat. "I heard you were here."

Her expression hardens instantly as she seems to get over my surprise arrival.

"What do you want?" she asks me, although it sounds like an interrogation. Before I can answer, she takes a half step forward to come outside rather than letting me in, like a fucking lunatic.

"What are you doing?" I ask her with complete disbelief as she tries to shut the door.

"I'm not having this conversation in Jules's house," Kat says as if it's an admonishment, like I'm the one who's lost their mind.

"Baby, get inside, it's freezing out!"

"Don't tell me what to do!" she yells back at me, and her words strike me across the face. I take it, though. I take one step back and watch as she crosses her arms over her chest and her cheeks quickly turn pink from the wind that won't let up, followed by the tip of her nose. "What do you want?"

"Are you sure you don't want to go inside?" I question her as calmly as I can, attempting to be reasonable.

"I went to your house today," she states. The blood drains from my face.

"Is that right?" I somehow manage to reply, knowing what's coming, my body tensing up. All I can hear is my heart pounding as I feel her slipping away from me.

"I don't want anything to do with you, Evan." The cutting words are spoken with a cracked voice. At least there's emotion left. If there's that, then I still have a chance.

"I don't know what you think you saw, but …" I start to tell her and then flinch from her shriek.

"Think?" she yells. "I saw her!" She moves in closer, getting in my face to scream at me. "Samantha. You left me to be with her," she says and seethes, the accusation coming out hard.

"Did you see me touch her?" I ask her, taking a step closer to her. "I know you didn't, because I never would. I'm not seeing her. I didn't even want her there."

"She was with you," she says the words then breathes out with nothing but pain and agony.

"Yeah, she was. A few times in the last week," I confess. I don't want her to find out any other way. "I'm trying to fix things and she's—"

"I want you to go," she says, cutting me off.

"I won't until you tell me you believe me." I look her in the eyes, silently begging her, and wait for it.

"I told you not to. Just go!"

"Never. I would never stray from you." As I say the words, it's crippling. Because I know she did what she's accusing me of. She's the one who's seeing someone else, but I gave her the space to do it. I left her side.

It's all fucked.

She doesn't answer me, merely shivers in the cold as her bottom lip starts to turn a purplish blue.

"Let's go inside," I urge her, but she doesn't respond. "I want to talk."

"I thought the funeral might be a good time to talk," she finally says with tears in her eyes. "Guess you didn't?

Her words slice through me, down to my core. "It meant a lot to me that you were there," I manage to say, but I can't look her in the eyes. The tips of my fingers turn numb and the feeling flows through every inch of my body.

"Didn't seem like it," she replies, although she's lost a bit of strength in her voice.

"I'm having a difficult time handling it," I tell her, scrambling for an excuse, but there's so much truth in those words.

James was there at the funeral. He even shook my hand, the fucking bastard. The reason is right there on the tip of my tongue. I wanted to go to her, to hold her.

To go home with her and get lost in her love. More than anything.

"You think it was easy for me?" she asks me after a moment of silence.

"You think it was easy for me?" I shoot right back and the memories of the grave, the service hit me. I have to pinch the bridge of my nose and close my eyes as I see the visions of the nightmares mixing with the memories. *I shouldn't even be here.* Regret flows through my veins. What am I doing?

"I'm sorry," she whispers, and her breath turns to fog. The wind blows, and her hair falls in front of her face as I tell her, "I'm sorry too." I get a little choked up, but I manage to tell her, "He loved you so much."

He really did. His voice telling me to make it right keeps playing in my head and it kills my strength.

"I told you I just needed time." I try to make the words come out strong, but instead, it's a plea. I don't know what to do anymore.

All I want to do is protect her. *Maybe that means losing her forever.*

She shakes her head. "What part of us moving on with our lives didn't you understand? I don't have time for games or whatever trouble you've gotten into."

"I'm fixing the trouble." I refuse to give up. "I just need more time."

"And how much longer is that going to be? How much longer do I have to sit on the back burner and wait for you to love me again?"

"I still love you," I say.

"You don't act like it."

"There's a reason for everything, I promise." I have to blink away the scenes of the funeral, of the night terrors.

"I don't want to hear your excuses anymore," she says and wipes under her eyes. Her voice is drenched with defeat. "You're supposed to be here for me."

I question everything in that moment. I'm so afraid of losing her, but the image of her dead on the ground makes me harden my resolve. I hesitate and immediately regret it.

"I need you to go, Evan. For good."

"It's because of Jacob, isn't it?" I can't help but blurt it out. I want someone else to blame. Someone else to hate other than me. "You're moving on with him?"

I can't help but point out that she's the one who wants someone else. I only want her. I won't lose her. I'll fuck her so good when all this is over, she'll forget any other man exists.

"You think I need a man? You think I need someone?" Her voice is coated with an anger I haven't seen from her before. "I never needed anyone! You're the only one I ever let in. You were the only one I let get close and I'll be fine, living the rest of my life alone."

"You want him more than me?" My jealousy gets the best of me.

"Get away from me!" she spits out as she opens the door to head into the house.

"I'm coming back for you," I tell her, and I mean it.

"Well I won't be here, and I'm changing the locks on the townhouse. So good fucking luck with that."

CHAPTER
nineteen

Kat

I**T'S A HEAVY, SINKING FEELING IN THE PIT OF YOUR** stomach. It rocks back and forth, making you queasy and your body can't sit still. That's what it feels like when you know you're about to hurt someone.

At least that's how it feels right now.

I don't need anyone at all and I don't want anyone either. Maybe I'm proving it to myself, or maybe to Evan. I don't care which.

My pulse quickens, and I try to swallow the spiked ball in my throat when I hear the bell at the front of the café.

Jacob smiles sweetly with genuine happiness as he strolls over to the table, letting his jacket slip off his shoulders. I'm going to miss that charming grin he has. I'll miss the comfort his presence brings more.

"One more nice day before winter comes in," he says easily. It's felt like winter for weeks now to me, but he's from farther up north, so I suppose it hasn't been as brutal to him as it's seemed to me.

"One more nice day," I repeat, nodding my head at the ceramic mug on the table. I have to force the smile to stay on my face, but it doesn't fool Jacob.

"What's wrong?" he asks me, not touching the mug of chai already waiting for him.

I hate that I get choked up. It's stupid really. Childish and I'm far too grown for little kid games.

It was just friends, then just a kiss.

But it never should have been anything.

"Nothing," I answer and shake my head slightly then pick up the mug. Jake's face falls, but he still tries to cheer me up.

"So, I never got your answer about the movies tomorrow night." He's quick to change the topic, gracing me with that ever-present kind smile. "I heard it's going to be good."

My mug clinks on the small saucer as he adds, "I love coffee shops and all, but it'd be nice to do something more."

More.

It would be. I can see it. I can feel it. If my heart didn't belong to someone else, I could see Jacob being so much more. Well, not only that. I'm going to be a mother. My priorities have nothing to do with dating or starting anything new that doesn't involve the little life I'm carrying.

"I have to tell you something." I get the words out before I change my mind and swallow them. Before I give in to getting over Evan by getting under another man.

Jacob visibly winces then scratches the side of his neck as he looks to the right. "That doesn't sound so good."

"I kind of lied to you," I confess, feeling a viselike grip on my heart.

"You're not separated?" he says.

"No, we are. But I don't want to be."

"You still love him. I know you do."

"There's more," I continue, not daring to look him in the eyes, and hesitate.

"Just tell me," he urges me as if this is going to be easy, moving his hand to mine, and I stare down at where his skin touches mine. It's gentle, kind. It's the comfort I desperately need. But I can't be expected to always have someone to lean on. More than that, I want to stand on my own.

"I'm pregnant," I tell him and the only reaction I get is that his brow raises just slightly. It's comical really, and the small movement forces the corners of my lips up. I'd laugh if my heart didn't hurt as much as it does.

"*That*, I didn't see coming," he responds, keeping a small bit of humor in his voice. Slowly, he pulls his hand away but keeps it on the tabletop. I notice the absence of his touch instantly, though.

"Not far along?" I shake my head no at his question, feeling the end of my ponytail swish around my shoulders. "How long have you known?"

"A while," I answer honestly.

"So that's the lie?"

"Yeah … I'm sorry. I never should have kept that from you."

"Don't be," he tells me and waves it off, as if it's no big deal.

"I knew better. It was just ..." I trail off and swallow my words, staring at a stain on the table. One that will never go away.

"It was nice being *okay* with someone. Right?"

I chance a peek up into his eyes. There's nothing but understanding there. "Yeah," I answer him and chew on my bottom lip. "I wanted to pretend to be okay for a little bit."

"Well it's not pretend," he continues and adjusts in his seat. "You can be okay if you want to." It's hard to hold his gaze as he brings his hand back to mine.

"Does he know?" I answer his question with a nod, my throat too tight to speak.

"And he ...?" he starts to ask, but doesn't finish the obvious question.

"Says he's happy but he's still not with me. He's not committing and carrying on like he was. I want him, but I need him with me and he's not ..." I'm ashamed of the answer.

It's quiet for a short moment. The ceramic mug in my hand slides against the wooden table and it's the only noise to be heard. The itch in my throat matches the prick behind my eyes. I've cried enough over all this. It's been weeks and this is simply how it is. With a sip of my peppermint tea, I accept it.

"So, do you want to go to the movies?" Jacob asks then picks up his mug. "I'd still like to go if you would."

My heart does this little flutter, a quick flicker of warmth that lets me know it's still there. It's gratitude and

I think that's all I could give anyone else. It's all I'm willing to do.

I shake my head, once again, and give him a sad smile.

"I had to ask. I think it would've been good," he tells me, forcing a smile then covering his disappointment by taking a large sip of the chai.

"You going to be okay?"

I shrug, honestly unsure of whether I'll ever be okay. "Some people are meant to be alone." *Or waiting for a love that may never come back.*

"You sound like me," he comments with a huff of humor that doesn't reach his eyes and then he takes a deep, heavy breath. "Gets tiresome, though."

"A story for another time perhaps?"

"I think it's the same story mostly, with only one big difference."

"What's that?"

"I think Evan may love you back, just like you love him. Whether or not he deserves it … well, that's a matter of opinion, I guess." I can't respond and instead, I let my gaze wander back to the stain on the table. "It wasn't the same for me. It was very much one sided."

"I'm so sorry, Jake." It's all I can respond and I genuinely am.

"Don't be," he says easily. "Fate puts people in our life for a reason." He takes a steadying breath before saying, "And now I know it's possible."

"What's possible?" For a moment I worry that he thinks the two of us being together is still an option when it's not at all for me.

"Not this like you and me," he says, rushing out the words as if hearing my unspoken thought. "Trust me, I wish it were. But I meant … just that there could be someone else for me."

"You could always write the story. Although I doubt you'd want me to be your agent, huh?"

"No … I don't think that would work really," he says with the same sad smile on his face that I've been giving him.

"Maybe we could still be friends?"

"I don't think that's for the best, Kat. I can't just be friends with you."

My hair tickles my shoulders as I nod and reach for my coat to leave. My movements are sluggish; I don't want this to be the last goodbye. But it is. I know it. I barely touched my drink and didn't have anything to eat, but that's okay. I knew I wouldn't anyway. Morning sickness has been rough this week so it's not like I'd be able to keep it down anyway.

"How about this," Jacob offers as I pull my wool coat tight around my shoulders. "You call me if you're ever not okay and want more. But I won't call you or text you again. It's in your hands."

"I'm sorry, Jake." I say the words, but they don't even make a dent in expressing what I feel.

"Stop being sorry. Do that one thing for me, will you?" he questions, his dark green, hazel eyes shining back just like they did the first moment I met him, and I merely nod and say my goodbye.

Every step back to my townhouse, I want to go back.

Every breath, I wish I could tell him that what he did for me, I can never repay, and I'll be forever thankful for that.

But neither of those things happen. I walk back to my townhouse alone and the first thing I do when I get home is delete his emails and his number.

I don't want to have the option to run back to him.

Jacob is a good man, but he's not for me. I don't need someone else to love me. I need to learn to love being alone again. So I can be whole for my child. So I can be a good mother.

Diary Entry Five

Dear Mom,

It's not so bad being alone. I'm not really alone, alone. Not with this baby growing, but I can't feel him or her yet. I still talk to him, though. I think it's a boy, but I won't know for weeks.

Like I said, though, I think it's going to be all right being alone for now. I remember having that same thought for a while after you guys left me. I know it's not your fault.

I just can't stand to think of needing someone. Not when it hurts so freaking bad when they leave you. Did you see what Evan did? I gave him that power and that's my fault. I won't do it again.

I should have known better.

If you could just remind me, maybe? The next time he comes around and says he wants me and that he loves me, can you give me a sign? Something that will remind me that he's just going to leave me again and how much that will hurt?

People don't change, and some people are meant to be alone.

I promise I'll be okay from now on, Mom.

I just forgot that I'm one of those people. But I remember now. I won't forget again.

CHAPTER
twenty

Evan

I'M USED TO SNEAKING AROUND. I'VE DONE IT ALL my life. I'm a professional at it, after all.

The door to the townhouse opens and I turn to look over my shoulder at the cold, barren street. No one knows I'm here and I need to keep it that way.

The pictures of my wife and me stare back at me as I slowly close the door. Feeling the warmth and familiarity of the home I built with Kat makes the ache deep in my chest twist and turn to a sickening degree. She took down several of our photographs, leaving dark rectangles on the wall where they used to hang and the sunlight failed to lighten and fade the paint behind them.

The large clock on the back wall ticks loudly as I move through the place we made together. It's nearly 3:00 a.m., but still, I make sure I wasn't followed. With bated breath, I check the surveillance system … again.

The life I led destroyed the only thing I ever had that I wanted to keep. My marriage.

The knowledge pushes me forward, each step bringing me closer to her. Closer to the bed we once shared, and closer to her warmth under the covers. As I push the door open, my heart beats slowly. With every second that passes my skin burns hotter and the worry threatens to consume me.

But the sight of her steady breathing and the faint movements of her body as Kat stirs in her sleep put all my worries behind me. She's safe, and that's what matters.

Her eyes flutter open and I stand as still as possible, terrified she'll see me, but she merely rolls over in bed, moaning slightly, pulling the thin white sheet with her.

The moonlight filters in through the curtains and leaves a trail of shadows that accentuate her curves as they fall across the bed. She's still as gorgeous as ever. Even in her sleep with no makeup on and her bare skin kissed by the faint light of the early morning, she holds a beauty that, for me, surpasses all others.

How many nights have passed with me failing to see that? How much time have I wasted?

I can't let a soul know I still love her. They'll use her to get back at me.

My eyes widen and my grip tightens on the door as I hear my name slip through her lips. "Evan." It sounded like a prayer, or maybe a plea. A soft moan escapes her as I take a hesitant step forward, wondering if she saw me or if I'm only with her in her dreams.

I start to question if she even said it, but then she says it again. The sweet sound of her soft cadence whispering my name is everything I need to keep going.

I swallow thickly, hating myself for what I've done and what I've put her through.

I dare to whisper the only thing that helps lure me to sleep at night, hoping it'll soothe her too, "I'll make it right, Kat. I promise, I'll make it right."

CHAPTER
twenty-one

Kat

MY EYES POP OPEN AT THE FAMILIAR CREAK from the stairs. My heart races faster and faster as I lie as still as I can, not daring to move a muscle. My body's hot and the covers are making me even hotter, but I don't move. I try not to even breathe as I wait for another sound. But nothing comes.

It's just my nerves. Maybe a nightmare.

Slowly, my breath comes back, but I'm still too scared to move. Nearly paralyzed still, I blink away the sleep and tilt my head just enough to look at the clock on my night-stand. 04:14 AM stares back at me in bright red digital numbers.

The sounds of the city streets filter in and my quick-ened heartbeat fades. It was nothing, I whisper and reach for my glass of water, downing it then wishing there was more.

Get up.

I will my body to move. I wince and crack my back, letting my bare feet hit the cold hardwood floor. Sleeping alone has never been a favorite of mine. Until Evan, I spent years with poor sleep patterns, both in falling and staying asleep. Even more than that, I don't like how Evan's side of the bed doesn't have the faint smell of him anymore. I can feel the solemn expression on my face as I glance at where he used to sleep, but it only pushes me to stand up straighter and wipe the sleep from my eyes.

The floor protests as I walk, and I let the feeling that someone was in here leave me. I have the security system … but I think I'd like a dog. *A big dog.*

The corners of my lips tip up into a smile as I walk down the stairs.

Pushing back the hair from my face, I slink down to the kitchen and turn on the light. It's early, but I'm starving. To sleep, or not to sleep becomes the question.

It only takes a glass of water, two Twinkies and a couple handfuls of grapes before I don't feel so hungry anymore and sleep is calling me upstairs again.

Passing through the dining room, I check over my shoulder just to make sure there's no one here. That eerie feeling still clings to me.

I think I'll name the dog Brutus. My lips purse as I wonder how dogs do with infants … I make a mental note to look that up first thing tomorrow.

I think I'm starting to really *feel* pregnant. It's beyond

being exhausted. It's something else, something that makes me rub my belly and talk to him or her as if they're already here. Some type of knowing and it makes me smile.

Before I can head back upstairs, my eyes catch sight of the flowers on the table. The flowers Jacob sent me when Henry died are already wilted. Bright yellow sunflowers. They're large and the stems are thick. They'll eventually die and by the look of them, that time is coming soon. What a shame ... that's what flowers do, though. They die.

Next to the vase is my laptop and I absently pull it toward the edge of the table then take a seat. My body aches, my hips especially, and sitting up feels better than lying down. I might as well get a little work in before I try to sleep again.

A yawn leaves me as the dim light of the computer brightens.

Studying the flowers again, I think about how twisted it is that I turned down a man who could have been perfect for me. A shrink might have something to say about that decision. My fingertips brush gently along the petals. I'll never know if we could have been more, but right now I'm content with that decision.

It's time I took control of my life.

My to-do list is already set. First step: I need a new place. Somewhere near the Manhattan Bridge, I think. It's far more family friendly. Dog friendly too.

I check my messages and emails, simply out of habit. A few of the candidates I picked to interview to be my personal assistant emailed me back. There are two of them I really like. I might actually hire both of them. Maybe that's really the first step. And then finding the perfect place will be step two. A smile plays across my lips and I nod to myself in approval of my "early morning can't sleep, aha" moment.

Those two tasks are momentous and huge leaps for me. Delegating work and settling down somewhere my child can have deep roots. Resting my hand on my belly, I promise I'll make it happen. I may have failed to be there for Evan, but for this baby, I'll do anything. I'll have it all fixed and ready before this one gets here. He or she will never know this place or all the hell that went on here.

My gaze drifts across the room and the night that started it all plays out in front of my eyes. Suddenly, it hurts. That numbing prick comes back. It's been happening like that. I'm so sure, so ready to move on … and then I remember. The visions of myself sitting there in the dining room chair like a ghost, drinking wine and wanting to deny it, and at the same time hating Evan because I knew he was lying.

A dreadful breath leaves me, and a sadness weighs down on my chest, but there's conviction there too.

A new place, a new way of life. My fingers drift to my belly button and then lower. A new life entirely.

Diary Entry Six

Hey Mom, can I take back what I said? I don't think I want to be alone.

I don't think alone is the right word. Alone hurts my heart a lot. It hurts more than I want to admit. Mom, it feels like the worst thing in the world sometimes. Now that I know what it's like to not be alone, I'm not sure that's really what I want.

I think that's why I clung to Jake. I just didn't want to be alone. You probably knew that, didn't you?

More than that, I want to be loved by someone who can love me the way I need and I can admit that.

How did you know Dad loved you the way you needed? I just laughed a little writing this. I'm sure he made it obvious. He didn't hurt you like Evan does to me.

I hope what Evan did doesn't make you mad. I don't think he means it. I think he doesn't know any better and I knew that when I married him.

Everything has settled now, and I know I want more, Mom. I really want someone to love me.

I want them to love me like Evan used to love me.

I don't know if it's possible.

I'm going to find someone one day. There's a lot to do between now and then, but I promise I won't settle for being alone.

Maybe not now. I don't know when. I'm not going to use them or compare them to Evan. It'll take time, but I think eventually I'll be able to do this.

This baby makes me feel loved and I know I love him or her.

I promise I'll give him every bit of love I have. A little extra too, lots of kisses from you. I know you'd love to hold him. I'll hold him extra tight for you. And for Henry. Henry would have loved this baby too.

CHAPTER
twenty-two

Evan

SHE TOOK OFF HER WEDDING RING TODAY.

I watched on a tiny-ass security monitor as she slipped it off and held it between her fingers. Miles away with the sins of the city between us, all I could do was watch her stare at it, as if wishing it would answer some unspoken question for her.

I hold my breath as I quietly open the door.

Kat didn't change the locks like she threatened to do, but that wouldn't have stopped me anyway.

This is the point that I've truly gone crazy and I know it. She's set boundaries and I don't give a shit about them. It's the first time in my life that's happened, but losing the woman you love will do that to a man. Watching her walk away when you know she loves you and you love her; it's a torture that's immeasurable and the destruction it leaves is irrefutable.

One slow step in, and not the faintest of sounds. The front door to the townhouse closes behind me softly. She'll forgive me one day. I'll hate myself forever if I stayed away.

Maybe I should have called, maybe I should have announced myself, but it's my home. She's my wife and this is where I belong.

I can accept that now. If I can keep secrets, so can Kat. I swallow thickly, closing my eyes and hating myself as I lock the front door. *She better be able to.*

I'm a desperate man. If anything happens to her, I'll end it. I already know that. But I'm so fucking weak that I'm risking it. If only she can keep a secret, we'll be all right.

My head whips around to the sound of the microwave beeping in the kitchen.

Beep, beep, beep followed by the click of the microwave being opened and a soft hum of satisfaction.

Kat. My love.

She's only a room away, and knowing what I'm about to do makes my heart race as I find it hard to swallow.

My body doesn't wait for me. My feet move on their own, pushing me closer to her. I need to see her, even if she doesn't see me. I can't explain why it needs to be in person.

The only light in the townhouse that's on is the kitchen light. It's early morning and I wasn't planning on her being awake.

Maybe the fact she's awake is a sign. A sign that I can't be a coward any longer.

That's what a man who waits in the shadows is. That's what a man who hurts his wife is. A fucking coward.

Stalking into the kitchen, I expect her to see me, but her back is turned as she stirs something in a bowl then slips it into the microwave, still humming something. It takes me a moment to realize it's a lullaby.

In nothing but a thin cotton sleep shirt, she tempts me.

Fuck, I've missed this view. When she raises her arms, the T-shirt she has on slips up past her thighs and gives me the smallest peek of her cheeks.

I almost groan from primal deprivation. It feels like forever since I've held her, laid her in bed and enjoyed her in every way possible.

"Kat." I say her name softly as the microwave starts and she whips around, backing into the cabinets with her hand on her chest.

"Sorry," I say and there's not a single second of hesitation when I apologize. "I know you said not to come … I just …"

I can see the outline of her breasts through the shirt and with her dark brunette hair a mess from sleep, she's never looked more beautiful. More fuckable. More *mine*.

"You scared the shit out of me," Kat whispers after a second, breathless.

"I'm sorry," I repeat. "I didn't mean to." I take a chance to move closer but stop at the kitchen counter. Boundaries. I've already broken so many of them. It's hard to keep my distance, but I'll wait.

"What are you doing here?" The microwave beeps and she rips the door open without taking the bowl out then slams it shut. Merely silencing it before crossing her arms over her chest.

I cock a brow at her anger, but she doesn't react.

"I brought these." Slipping my hand into my jacket pocket, I pull out the pair of baby shoes I got from home. They're the same pair I wore when I was little. Smooth leather and simple, but before me, they were my father's. I found them in a box in Pops's basement. Ma put them there. It's her handwriting.

Kat pinches the bridge of her nose and turns her shoulder to me, hiding her expression, but I saw it. The sweep of sadness cuts me to my core.

"Baby?" I whisper softly, cautiously even. "I—"

"What are you doing?" she says, cutting me off as she stares daggers in my direction.

"I know you're angry." My tone is placating, but it does nothing to soothe her.

"Angry doesn't even begin to cover it."

A second passes, followed by another as I struggle to form the right words. "I have faith you'll forgive me," I tell her with feigned confidence.

"Fuck off," she spits out.

"Because you love me. And you know I love you."

"You love me?" she questions with a deep scowl. Storming toward me, she sticks her finger in my chest as she yells. "This is what love is?" She shoves me back and I take it, loving the fight in her. But it doesn't last long.

"Your father died, and I had to be alone." She murmurs

the truth I already know and takes a step back. "You chose to be alone," she whispers. She tries turning from me again, but I grip her waist.

"I didn't want it to be like that. I swear to you." Bringing up my pops hits me hard. I keep forgetting and that's how I want it to be. I keep thinking he'll call or text. I keep thinking when all this is over, we'll have dinner together on Sundays again. I hate it when I remember he's not here anymore. I can't handle losing them both at once.

"I'm not all right." I whisper the truth to her as something pricks at the back of my eyes. "I'm sorry." Sincerity is there, but I don't know that she can hear it anymore. The feeling of worthlessness washes over me.

"Sorry doesn't cut it." She takes in a deep breath meant to steady her, but it seems to do the opposite.

"You know what loving you means?" I ask her, raising my voice. "It means protecting you."

"You can take all those words and—"

"They're in my vows," I say, heaving out the words as I interrupt her, my emotions rising and the thought of losing Kat forever becoming more and more real. "Protecting you is in my vows."

"Don't talk to me about vows." I've never seen her so angry. The look in her eyes is pure hate mixed with mourning.

"Come here," I tell her and her eyes narrow.

She tilts her head to the side and looks at me as if I've lost my mind. My heart feels like it does a somersault, a painful flip in my chest as she says, "Don't tell me what to do."

"The only reason I've been gone is that being seen with you would put you in danger." I hate myself the moment the confession slips out. Weak. I'm so fucking weak. I need to be a better man for her, but I've never been good enough and we both know that.

Kat's silent, but her expression is unchanged.

With a hesitant step forward and my hands held out to her, I add, "I had to do it."

"You don't have to do a damn thing but breathe," she finally responds, her voice hollow, the devastation I've caused ringing out clearly.

"I was only trying to keep you safe." I say the words quietly as the sight of Kat in front of me becomes more of a reality than my fear ever was.

She hates me. I've made my wife hate me. Pain ricochets through every piece of me.

"Well, thank you for that," she answers sarcastically with tears in her eyes as she shakes her head.

"I swear." I feel tears prick my eyes as I fall to my knees in front of her. I'm not in control anymore. I'm not in control of a damn thing and purely at her mercy. "I'm here right now because I can't stay away any longer." My heart crumples at the words that I choke on.

Kat takes a small step back, brushing against the counter as she does, and I wish I still had a grip on her.

I murmur my apology. "I didn't know it would take this long. I'm sorry. I fucked up. Repeatedly and I'm trying, but I'm failing."

"Didn't know what would take this long?" she asks, crossing her arms and refusing to look into my eyes, but she's full of emotion and on edge waiting for me to open up to her. I know her, and I know that's exactly what this is. That's what made her fall in love with me. I swallow the thick lump in my throat and pray I'm not making a mistake.

"I'm …" I can hardly breathe as the words *threatening, investigating, framing* get caught in my throat.

"Tell me, Evan." Kat licks her lower lip and stares down at me with tired eyes. "I've had enough and I'm over the secrets and the lies. I'm over this," she says and gestures between us although as she does, her expression morphs into pain. "What was so important that it had to be done to protect me?"

"It's going to sound crazy," I warn her, staring up at her from where I am as the dawn slips in through the windows, playing with the shadows on her gorgeous face.

"It already does."

"James is the one who's responsible for Tony's death." I confess still on my knees, although I let go of her. I hate myself for telling her and bringing her into this, and I almost don't say another word.

"He was trying to kill me, not Tony." My throat is dry and scratchy as the words slowly leave me and I rise to stand, feeling the weight of it all rain down on me. "And he knows I know."

Denial forces Kat to shake her head, a crease settling between her brow. It's a small motion of disbelief, but she doesn't speak as she drops her arms, listening.

"It's because of his divorce. He wants Samantha scared and he wanted to prove he'd do anything. So he tried to kill me, thinking I'd do a line of it. It backfired."

Her mouth opens and closes, but she still says nothing. A lightness carries me forward, knowing she's listening. At the very least, she's listening.

Please believe me. "I've been tracking his schedule and routines, breaking into his house and office looking for evidence or something that can prove it."

A huff of disbelief so faint I almost think I imagine it leaves Kat's lips as she turns from me, facing the sink and putting her fingers to her lips.

"Talk to me, please," I beg her and a trace of anger flashes in her eyes.

"You could have gone to the cops," she finally says. "Like a normal human being."

"I couldn't go to the cops with nothing on him. James has proof I was with Tony. It's his word against mine, and he has photos. I listened to him that night. I went along with the alibi and lied to the cops. I fucked up and he tried to blackmail me, but I called his bluff."

"Jesus Christ," Kat says then exhales.

"You see why I didn't tell you? It's too much and you're pregnant. If he's after me and he knows I love you, he'd go after you too." My biggest fear slips from me and I can't control how my eyes glaze over as the terrors I've dealt with every night for weeks linger between us. I've pictured her here on the floor, just by my feet, dead almost every night.

Yet I'm here. I've told her. And there's a chance I just brought that reality to life.

"You could have messaged me; you didn't have to hurt me."

Swallowing thickly, I gather my composure, refusing to let the fear win although everything else has failed. "He's tracking my texts, babe, he's following my every step. Just to get here, I had to make sure to lose the guy he paid to follow me around."

"This is insane, Evan. You know that, don't you?"

"I know, and I'm sorry. I have someone working on it and we're trying."

"Who?" she asks and when I don't answer she adds, "No more secrets, and no more lies. I want all of it."

"Mason," I confide in her, and it takes a moment to register.

"Does Jules know?" she asks, worry riddled in her downturned expression.

"I doubt it."

"So, because you think I could have been in potential danger, you left me alone, treated me like I was … like I was nothing?"

"He would have killed you," I tell her, stressing the truth of the situation.

"You don't know that."

"I met him, and he brought you up." My throat goes dry at the memory. "He would have gone for you, Kat."

She shakes her head in disbelief.

"If I lose you, I have nothing!" The words are ripped from my throat, desperate for her to see what I've been seeing. To feel what I've been feeling, complete and utter loss. I calm my voice and take a step closer to her then say, "If he killed you, I would have nothing to live for."

She stares into my eyes with a look I can't quite read

and whispers, "I'd rather die beside you than live without you."

"I would kill myself if anyone hurt you because of me. I don't know how you can't see that." She appraises me for a moment, her shoulders rising and falling with soft breaths. "I promise it's almost over. I promise you Kat, I wouldn't do this if I didn't have to."

"You should have known better than to keep it from me. What if you had died?" she asks me, and I can't answer right away. I'd never considered it. "What if he killed you? I would have never known."

"My only thought was to keep you safe; I wasn't concerned with anything else.

"If you do what I say, we can still be together," I tell her and the reaction I get is nothing like what I'd planned. She's not at all moved by my confession. She can't tell a soul or let on that we're together. "If we're together," I say then stop midsentence, afraid that we're not. Afraid that it's too late.

"You don't control me anymore." Although her words are spoken easily, and she seems to understand everything, her walls are still high, guarding her from me.

"Kat, I love you, but I will lock you in a fucking room to keep you safe. If you don't listen to me, then you leave me with no choice. I swear to God I will."

Smack!

My face burns with a stinging sensation as the sound rings in the air. My lungs halt as my eyes widen, taking in the vision of a pissed-off Kat in front of me with her hand still raised. My hand slowly rises to my jaw.

I've never seen Kat strike a person in my life. She's not a violent person by nature.

But I guess I had it coming to me.

"Don't you dare tell me that you love me."

I don't fucking hesitate to respond, "I love you more than anything, and I'll never deny it. I'll tell you every single day for the rest of my life." Even with my jaw stinging from the impact.

"I can keep a secret too. You could have told me. You didn't have to put me through this with everything else I'm dealing with."

"One slip is all it will take. If anyone even thinks we're back together … that's all it would take."

"Well, you told me now," she states with finality and I take her hand in mine, forcing it up so she can see.

"Because you took off your ring," I tell her, not holding back the pain it caused. "Because you kissed someone else." Her fight vanishes, not all at once, but slowly as both of us breathe heavily, the air between us growing hotter. "Because I thought I was losing you forever."

"You left me with no choice," she says although a look of regret flashes in her eyes.

"I didn't have one either. You have to believe me."

"You really love me?"

"I do. You must know it's true. I know you do."

"You want to be with me? You want to keep me yours?" she asks, completely serious as if there's any other option for me.

"Yes, it's all I want. And to keep you safe."

"Evan." She utters my name softly but as it rings

through the air, I hear the threat that comes with it. Her eyes pierce through me as she stares back at me.

"You'll come back to me, every night. Every fucking night. You'll message me back every time I text you."

"I can't text you back from my phone." Her eyes narrow and I'm quick to come up with a solution as I offer, "But I can get another."

"Damn right you will," she answers me and I find the corners of my lips kick up in amusement. I love my wife and she loves me. *Thank fuck.*

Just as that truth begins to comfort me, she adds, "I don't like you doing this."

"I promise it's almost over."

"Evan, you better never do this to me again."

"I promise, baby. I promise never again. Everything's going to change from here on out. I promise."

"We can get through anything, but never this again," she whispers, and I know I have her. I have her back and I'll be damned if I ever let her feel lonely again.

CHAPTER
twenty-three

Kat

"Talk to me," Evan says again, and I want to. God, I do, but there's so much to say.

"You want to hear what I've been wanting to tell you for weeks?" I ask and even to my own ears, I sound like I've lost it.

"Kat, you—"

I don't care what he has to say, I'm going to lay it all out there for him and he can decide what he wants to do with it. I have a plan, I have needs. Either he's in, or he's out. I'll accept either; I'm willing to give it a chance. There's only so much that's left of me, though, and he needs to be very aware of that.

"I'm exasperated. Just because you said sorry doesn't

take away everything. It doesn't make it all just fine and back to normal. I'm still … *feeling*." The spiraling that's come over me day in and day out threatens to take me over now, and I let it happen. "I feel like someone's run over my body with a truck and then backed up. My hips and back hurt. I can't sleep. And that's just the pregnancy." With a deep inhale, I continue before he can interrupt me.

"You know, the baby you put in me? That's still happening and by the way, pregnancy doesn't just pause because things have been insane. So, I'm dealing with hormones, and I cry way too much for no reason. I feel sick and I can't sleep. I'm paranoid and I'm so damn alone that I've truly been scared. I feel crazy and I don't even know what part of this is normal and what part isn't." The words leave me in a fluid mix of emotions. Like a purge of everything I've been feeling, piling up until it drowned me. With a shuddering breath, I attempt to calm myself, not knowing how he'll take any of it and very much aware I'm an absolute mess.

After a moment, he speaks. "I want to hold you," is all he says. I'm caught, shaken and uncertain as I stand in front of him in nothing but a T-shirt in our kitchen. My God do I want him, but murder? People trying to kill him? I can barely handle normal life. "I want to make all the pain go away; I'll take it from you. I promise," he says in a deep cadence that washes a sense of calm over it all. Evan slips closer to me, wrapping a hand around my waist and I can feel myself falling back into the same trap. Because he does that to me. He makes the pain go away and he makes it so easy to give in.

"Stop," I say, pleading with him. "It's like history repeating itself." My body and my thoughts are at war with each other. I'm brought back to every kiss we've had, every time he's held my hand, every heated moment that's left me consumed. The world is nothing without him in it and I know it, mind, body and soul.

"It's not," Evan says matter-of-factly to me, his voice begging me and my body persuading me to once again fall into his arms. Which is right where I want to be. The very thought tugs at every string wrapped around my battered heart.

"We have a baby coming and I can't put this baby through what we've been going through, Evan," I say, admitting my fears to him. If only he knew how much it hurt. "I'm afraid every time I cry the baby can feel it. I terrified I'm hurting him already." As I say the words, tears prick my eyes.

"Him?" Evan asks. "You think we're having a boy?" The shine in his eyes is of pure devotion. That's how he breaks me down. By truly loving me.

"Don't change the subject," I warn him although it warms my heart and I can't help but feel it resonate. "I want you, Evan. But I want you here with me, and committed to me and this baby."

"I know," he says. "I love you, Kat. I love you with everything in me and I won't stop proving that to you every day for the rest of our lives."

Even though he's saying all the right things and I love it, I have to be honest. "I swear I can't take it anymore."

"Never again. I can't stand not being with you," he tells

me, and my body succumbs to a warmth that's been there all along, waiting just beneath the surface.

He pulls me into his arms and I let him. Even more, I grip onto his shirt as he wraps his muscular arms around me and I breathe in his scent of fresh forest after rain. This is home. This is what feeling complete feels like. I'm so very aware of everything he said only moments ago. The threats and danger are legitimate, but it all comes with him. I can keep a secret. I'll do whatever I have to if it means I get to have Evan completely.

My eyes shut tight, willing the unwanted thoughts away as Evan whispers just beneath the shell of my ear, "I want to make it all better." He's so close that my hair tickles my neck as it moves gently with his breath.

He says the right words. He's always been good at that.

He lowers his lips to the sensitive part of my neck. "I only want to love you, and have you love me back."

My poor heart has barely survived all this time without him, but it rages now, pounding against my rib cage. I suppose it's only beating still because it hasn't belonged to me in years. *It's always been his.*

I nod my head and look down at his chest, inhaling his scent I've missed for so long, feeling his touch I've been craving.

"You're still wearing your jacket," I comment softly as I run the tips of my fingers down the zipper. I lift my gaze to his dark eyes, swirling with desire. "Take it off."

I bite my lower lip then take half a step back as he keeps his eyes on mine and slips his jacket down his arms.

"Your shirt," I say in a breathy voice and in an instant,

he tugs it over his head then carelessly drops it to the floor. The fabric puddles at his feet. He closes the space between us as desire spikes in my blood. Like the first night I saw him, knowing he was trouble, yet I can't resist.

"What now?" Evan asks, moving his pointer finger to the bottom of the cotton T-shirt and slipping it upward, tugging ever so gently until he reaches the peaks of my breasts. He closes his fingers around my nipples with a slight pinch and then tugs. Gasping, I let my head fall back. The sensation is directly linked to my clit and it forces me to part my lips with a soft moan. "What now, baby?"

"Mmm," I manage, and that's all I can offer as lust clouds my judgment. I missed this. I missed him. Such a small touch and yet it feels all-consuming.

"How about this?" Evan suggests and then he unbuckles his belt. The sound of his pants being unzipped fills the small kitchen and my body aches to reach out to him.

His pants fall to the floor and he pushes his boxers down with them, stepping out of them and exposing his already hard cock. Every nerve ending in my body lights just seeing him bared to me. Knowing how much pleasure he can and will give to me.

A rough chuckle distracts me from focusing on his erection and I look into his eyes.

"You still want me?" he asks and it's only then that my cheeks warm with a blush. My body sways slightly. I murmur my answer. "Always."

Evan runs the same pointer finger along my upper thigh past my panties and traces the center seam of the cotton, brushing my throbbing clit and sending sparks of heated pleasure through my body. My body leans forward, my hands gripping onto his corded forearms.

"I will never risk making you unhappy again. I promise," he says. My head is so dizzy with desire, I can only moan in response.

"Tell me," he says as he slides his fingers under the thin fabric and runs them along my hot core. He pushes against my clit with just the right amount of pressure then nearly slips into me as he runs his fingers back down. My hands fly up to his chest, gripping onto him for balance as my toes curl and my body begs me to ride his fingers.

"Tell me," he repeats then stops. My heavy-lidded eyes open, and I pull back to object. "Tell me you still want me."

"I still want you," I whisper without hesitation; the words rush out of my lips with need and desperation. Before the last word is even spoken, Evan splays his hand on my lower back and pulls me closer to him, forcing my chest against his.

"Fuck, you're so wet," he groans in the crook of my neck as he forces two fingers deep inside of me. I cry out in pleasure, clinging to him as the sensation nearly topples me.

"Evan." I moan out his name, but he doesn't answer as the pleasure builds. It's been so long but I don't remember it ever being like this.

It's so intense, so overwhelming that I know I can't remain standing for this.

"Evan," I plead for him to understand, but my head flies back and strangled moans fill the air, both from him and from me as I find my release on his fingers.

My body buckles and shakes as the orgasm rocks through me. I'm paralyzed as Evan moves me to the counter. It's cold and hard, and I lean against it for balance as slow waves mercilessly continue to flow through my body.

"And your shirt?" Evan asks me as if I didn't just experience the strongest orgasm of my life.

I grip the counter tightly while I catch my breath, staring at him.

"I want it off," he commands and with my back to his chest, he tugs the shirt off me. My body sways easily, caving to his every whim. "And these," he tells me, pushing his hand back down my panties. I'm trapped with my back to his front and his strong arm pinning me to him, his other hand on my hip, keeping me still.

My fingers clutch at his wrist and my blunt nails dig into his flesh as he strums my sensitive clit.

"Evan." His name is a plea as my body falls forward, and I struggle to take more.

He's not gentle with his strokes in the least. And I love it. My nipples pebble and my body goes weak with a numbing, blinding intensity.

The pleasure stirs deep in my belly, but like a flame it grows hotter and hotter, warming me and threatening just the same.

It's only when I come again that Evan slowly pulls my panties from me, leaving them by my feet. I'm not blind to the fact that they're damp with my desire.

Evan moves his hard erection between my thighs and I widen my stance slightly. He kisses my ear as he runs the head of his dick up and down my folds. A shiver runs through my body. Every inch is covered with a heated pleasure so sensitive to touch, that I shudder from just his hot breath on my neck.

"I love you, Kat," Evan whispers as he pushes himself deep inside of me. Slowly, stretching my walls. My head falls back onto his shoulder as he wraps his arm in front of me, holding me to him. He reaches up and grabs my throat.

Buried deep inside of me, he whispers, "Tell me you love me."

"Always," I say and the word slips out easily, my eyes still closed. I slowly open them to see Evan's expression. I'm struck by the intensity of his gaze. The need, the desire, the possession. "Say the words," he commands.

"I'll always love you," I tell him softly, the words barely audible.

He crushes his lips against mine as he bucks his hips. The sudden spike of near pain makes me push my head back and scratch along his forearm. He doesn't stop pounding into me, letting the pleasure build.

He pistons his hips relentlessly, each thrust forcing a pleasured groan from me. I try not to make too much noise, I try to be quiet, but I can't.

I come again and again, each climax feeling more intense than the last. Evan's ravenous as he kisses me. He doesn't stop his hands roaming over my body. He doesn't stop until I have nothing left, and only then does he bury himself in me to the hilt and find his own release.

Diary Entry Seven

Mom,

I think I've lost my mind.

Evan's like a tornado in my life.

That's not news to you, but I think that's how I want it. Crazy and reckless, but deeply rooted and unstoppable.

I'm ready to fight for him, Mom. For us. I'm eager to, even.

I love him. I love what he does to me when he's with me.

Mom, I'm afraid you'd be ashamed of me if you were still here. That's the only part that hurts.

But believe me when I tell you that I love him and in all his fucked-upness, he loves me.

That hole I was telling you about before? It's the one that came when you left, but it's not there when Evan's with me.

I think he has a hole in his heart too, Mom.

And I think I'm the only one that can fill it.

I told you I've gone crazy, didn't I?

Maybe it's not the worst thing in the world, though. I don't know. I don't think I care about it much anymore. So long as I keep Evan close to me.

I hope I make you proud. And if not, I'm sorry, Mom. I didn't choose this, but I choose him. I want to see it through.

CHAPTER
twenty-four

Evan

The paper rustles in my hand. It's a list Pops left on the counter. He didn't tell me about it, but I'm sure it was for us.

Bottles.

Pacifiers.

Bibs.

Onesies.

It goes on for a bit, but it's everything I need to buy. I'm not sure if he was going to give it to me, or if he was going to get this all himself. A pain radiates in my chest, right where that beating organ is. I miss him. I've never needed to talk to him as much as I do now.

You have to do it. I read the text that buzzes through and then put both my phone and the list in my pocket. I already know what Mason is getting at.

He's convinced I need to be seen in public. To make sure the tail James has on me sees me keeping my distance, moving on. He wants them to back off and that means I need to look like I'm backing off too. No more of this tit for tat. The plan is to let them think I've moved on from looking into James. That I've given up or simply decided it wasn't worth it. It doesn't matter which.

I stare down the aisle as a kid runs past, holding up a plane in the air and making swooshing noises. It's crazy that one day, I'm going to have one of them. A kid. A baby first. And before that, a pregnant wife.

It's fucking terrifying.

This particular setting isn't what he had in mind and I made sure no one followed me here. Family first, though, and then I'll take care of the mess. Bars and old hangouts. Then back to the apartment every night before I sneak out to go home. She's a saint for putting up with me and all of this.

"Hey," I call out as a young guy in a blue Kiddie Korner T-shirt walks by with a clipboard in his hand. He has to push his glasses up the bridge of his nose when he looks at me. "Can I help you, sir?"

"Yeah, I was looking for simple baby things. Like bottles and tiny clothes. Things like that," I tell him. "I can't find them anywhere in here."

"We don't have infant merchandise. You'll have to go to Little Treasures," he responds and starts walking to the center of the store to point. "Two blocks down and make a right. It's a bit of a walk, but it's right there on your left."

"Thanks."

I rub my tired eyes and walk out of the shop, hearing the ding of bells above my head and I'm instantly accosted by the bitter cold.

Just as I'm shoving my hands into my pockets, I catch sight of Detective Bradshaw.

"It's one of those days," I mutter under my breath as he kicks off the wall. Guess the prick was waiting for me.

"Mr. Thompson," he says, greeting me without a hint of emotion as he closes the distance between us.

I take a few steps forward as a couple of kids run behind me and into the store. Meeting him halfway, I answer him, "Detective Bradshaw, nice to see you again." *Not fucking really.*

He huffs a laugh like he heard my thought and says, "I'm glad I found you here."

"A bit odd that we just happened to run into each other." Holding his gaze, I let him know that I know he must've been following me. "Not my usual hangout."

"Yeah, I noticed. Your schedule's a bit different now?"

"A bit."

"For the best, I hope?" he asks and a prickle runs down my neck. I don't like it.

"Yeah," I answer, and my word comes out hard. My back's stiff and my muscles are wound tight. "You taking me in?"

I wait as he assesses me, enjoying the suspense.

"Should I?"

"I can't think of any reason off the top of my head." He doesn't think my answer's funny in the least. My lips quirk up into a smirk at his hard-assed expression. "I'm good to go then?"

"You got any new information for me?" he asks, getting to the point of this meeting.

"I got nothing to say."

"Why are you doing this to yourself? Protecting someone who wants to issue harassment charges?" he asks me, and I can't help that my forehead creases with both confusion and anger.

"Oh," Detective Bradshaw says, finally showing a little joy. "You didn't hear?" He rocks on his feet like he's happy to deliver the news. "James Lapour wants us to keep you away from him. He filed for a restraining order and all."

"That's why you're here?" I ask, not sure what to make of James's move. He went to the cops and maybe I grew up different, but that's something you just don't do when you're neck-deep in criminal shit.

"He said you were snooping around, making him uncomfortable and issuing threats."

"Threats?" I echo, getting more pissed off by the second.

"Nothing solid we could work with, so I thought I'd give you a shadow."

"Ah, and thus this wonderful meeting." I don't talk to cops. Never have, never will. Half the city's cops are in someone's back pocket. *Someone's* like Mason and James; the rich *someone's*. Not *someone's* like me and the kids I grew up with.

"I'm sorry to say I couldn't really give two shits about James Lapour so if you want me to stay away, I'm happy to keep my distance."

Detective Bradshaw's less than pleased with my statement. "Just thought you'd like to know."

"Thanks, Detective, am I good to go now?"

"Have a good day," he mutters as he walks past me, brushing my shoulder as he goes.

I finally bring my hands out of my pocket and open my clenched fist only to see the scrap of paper balled up. My breathing comes in shorter and my blood heats.

This shit has to stop. Right fucking now.

Diary Entry Two

Dear Pops,

I'm ashamed. I feel like I've lost complete control and I know it's hurt Kat.

Help me to be a better husband and take the nightmares away. Please. Just get them out of my head.

It's just getting worse every night, and it's scaring my wife.

What kind of a man am I? Dreams are tearing my life apart.

I can't sleep without seeing you. Don't get me wrong, I love and miss you so damn much, but you always die in my dreams. You're gone. All of the memories of our life together are changing. I don't want them to, but I don't know how to stop it.

I have them with Kat too, and it's killing me.

I yelled in my sleep last night, and it woke me up. Kat was crying next to me, Pops. She said she'd been trying to wake me up and that's when I started screaming.

She's worried, and I feel like less of a man and husband because I can't stop it.

Please, Pops, if you're there and you're able to, please help me.

I miss you. I can't stand this.

Please just take it all back.

Kat

AT WHAT POINT DID THIS BECOME MY LIFE?

I've been asking myself that question all morning. I've showered, I've eaten and cleaned most of the townhouse. But my mind is fuzzy with disbelief.

A sigh leaves me at the thought as I hail a taxi just outside our townhouse. The winter weather has lightened up some, and I almost feel like I could wear a light jacket and not this heavy wool coat. Maybe I've just gotten used to the cold.

It doesn't take long for a yellow and black cab to pull to a stop in front of me. Ushering myself in, my mind still fails to grasp all the details of everything that's happened in only months.

If an author submitted my story to me as a manu-script, I'd tell them it's too unbelievable. What's that quote from Mark Twain? Something about how truth is stranger than fiction because fiction needs to make sense.

"Where to, miss?" the cabby asks me as I get in the back seat and close the door.

"Saks on Fifth, please," I answer confidently, although my nerves creep up. Evan would kill me if he knew what I was doing, but it's not going to stop me. I need this.

There are only two things I'm certain of.

1. I can't afford to let Evan leave me again or else I'll truly lose my mind.
2. I'm not going to stay out of this like Evan wants.

The car moves forward, taking me away from the empty townhouse. He's gone off to meet with Mason and tell him what we agreed on. He's staying with me, commit-ting to me and our baby. And he promised to move past this. I'll listen to what he tells me to do, but every night he comes back to me and sleeps with me in our bed. No more secrets and hiding. I have to help him, not let the fear of what might happen ruin what we have in the present.

I'm still pissed that Mason knew when I didn't. It's the second knife in my back, but I let it slide simply because it's not his ring on my finger.

Instead, I focus on the real target here. Samantha Lapour. I'm not over her being with him when we were separated. The hate and jealousy are still there.

She loves Fifth Avenue. What rich New York socialite doesn't?

I remember her bragging about her apartment above Saks when I first met her. She was so happy to keep it even though she and her husband were happily married. It wasn't so much a humblebrag as it was just bragging.

That should've been my first clue we were never destined to become friends, but her smile was charming and her stories were alluring. I'll admit, I was dazzled.

The cabby stops before I'm ready, my nerves getting the best of me, and it's only then that the weight of what I'm doing makes my stomach churn.

I pay the cabby, slipping out and onto the curb to avoid the traffic.

My pulse races faster and faster, adrenaline surging as I make my way through the throngs of people and into the apartment foyer, disappearing from the crowd and readying myself to knock on her door on the fourteenth floor.

I don't know the exact address, though. There are only so many up here, so if at first I don't succeed, I'll simply try again.

My legs are shaky as I climb the stairs; I should have taken the elevator. Some small part of me is quite aware that the decision was made to eat up time.

"Good evening," a feminine voice says, and I have to raise my gaze to watch an older woman with a stylish white bob and a small Pomeranian in her arms close the door to 1401. There are only two other apartments on this floor, the one I'm sure Samantha told me about.

But that was years ago …

"How are you?" I greet the woman as if I'm supposed to be here, as if I'm visiting a friend and not a woman I have every intention of warning to stay the hell away from me and my family. In an effort to be convincing, I open my clutch, keeping my eyes on her with a simper plastered on my face. I'm sure it looks like I'm getting out a key or maybe my phone to call a friend.

The woman simply smiles tightly and nods then carries on her way, not answering the question. I hesitate, glancing between the remaining two doors and wondering which one I should knock on first.

This is crazy.

My heart races and a mix of adrenaline and anxiousness make me question why I'm even here.

The real answer, the absolute truth, hisses in the back of my head.

She was with him. In his family house.

Two confident strides and I knock, one, two, three times on 1402. I don't breathe until I take a small step back and wait.

Silence. No response. The confidence threatens to leave with every second that passes, but the moment I take a step to the right, to knock on the only other option, the door opens.

In red silk pajamas and her hair in curlers, Samantha looks so different from any other time I've seen her. She wasn't expecting company, that's for sure.

Her expression is nothing but irritation at first, and then she recognizes me.

"Oh, hello," she says, greeting me somewhat easily but with her lips pressed in a thin straight line as she stands up straighter. "Kat."

I have to clear my throat before I can answer her. "Samantha," I respond in the same stiff way. "I apologize for dropping by with no notice. I was hoping I could talk to you." Clutching my purse with both hands in front of me, I add, "It's about Evan."

She crosses her arms, instantly on the defensive and I'm quick to add, putting on a bit of a show, "I'm worried about him. About the loss of his father and how he's handling it." The words are the truth and the emotion that comes with them is genuine. But I just want an in so I can get a better grip on exactly who this woman is ... and maybe details on her estranged husband.

"I'm so sorry for your loss," she responds tightly, still looking me up and down as she considers what to do with me.

"I know you've spent a little time with him and I was just hoping you could tell me how he is."

She nearly flinches then has to take a moment before she can answer. As if she has no idea how he's doing. Or maybe she's shocked that I know she's seen him, but it's all over the papers, so why wouldn't I?

Evan's told me one side of this story, but there are always three sides ... sometimes even more. In this case I'll stay away from James, for Evan's sanity, but I'm sure Samantha will have a thing or two to gossip about.

"Did you guys talk at all?" I ask her. My throat tightens as I add, "He doesn't talk to me at all anymore."

"Oh, God," Samantha says, sounding exasperated and then tells me, "We didn't talk about his father. I'm sorry." She struggles to gather a response. "I'm sure it's difficult and I understand you two are going through something, but I assure you that I'd like to stay out of it."

With the creak of the heavy door, she attempts to close it, but I'm quicker.

My palm smacks against the door and I plead with her, "I just need someone to talk to. Please! If you could just let me in."

My blood rushes in my ears as I wait, the door remaining right where it is, only slightly cracked. She opens it again cautiously, pursing her lips and appearing more irked than anything else. As she lets go of the door, it opens with my weight and she nods her head, letting me in.

"What is it that you want?" she questions as she walks with her back to me inside of the apartment. I close the front door myself and take the place in.

It's a barren disaster.

I nearly ask her if she was robbed, but looking to my left at a cluttered kitchen I can easily spot a potential cause of the state of her place. Three small bags of white powder and a line wait for her. Right next to them is a colorful bag of pills. A mix of what could be Adderall and pain meds.

She turns with a smirk on her lips. "Like the place?" she asks sarcastically. "My prick of an ex made sure to sell all my belongings when I went out of town."

"Oh my God," I say, the words coming out in a whisper of disbelief and pity, neither of which truly resonate with me. There's only a sofa in the living room, a sleek gray contemporary sectional. I imagine it would look beautiful if the living room itself wasn't devoid of any other piece of furniture. She settles down onto one end and I take the other.

Glancing up at the chandelier I tell her, "I'm so sorry. I'm sure it was beautiful ..." my voice trails off and she doesn't say anything.

"You could go to the cops," I offer her, and she laughs with ridicule. If she weren't so arrogant, I'd feel sorry for her. With her cheeks sunken in and the silk pajamas baggy on her slim frame, she appears far less beautiful and enviable than I remember her.

"He's got them all on payroll, sweetheart. I'm barely surviving."

"I am so sorry," I say, at a loss for words and feeling so much more uncomfortable than I anticipated. I even feel bad for her to some degree.

"Divorce isn't always a bad thing, love," she says and then takes in my expression. "I'm sorry for you two, though, I really am."

It's hard to judge her tone, so I'm not sure how to take it.

"I actually had something to ask you about your husband." I shift on the sofa, preparing to question her. Samantha reaches for a pack of cigarettes and slips one out.

She lights it then asks, "What's that?"

There's a glint in her eyes and her back stiffens slightly.

"Evan doesn't like him much anymore," I offer her, gauging her reaction and she lets out a small laugh that's accompanied by smoke.

"I don't much like the asshole either."

"Can't blame you," I say, keeping my tone agreeable as I set my purse down beside me and feign a casualness I don't feel.

"He told me weeks ago he thinks James is trying to hurt him." I hold her gaze as I say, "I think he's paranoid, but he's worried about his reputation since leaving the company."

Samantha takes a long drag of her cigarette, ignoring the question until I tell her.

"I was hoping that if I talked to you, you could tell me the truth. Evan's just being crazy, isn't he?"

Every nerve is on edge in my body. There's something about how she looks at me. It's as if she's wondering what to do with me.

I don't trust the look, and I don't trust her.

"Evan told you what, exactly?"

"Evan told me that James tried to kill him, thinking he'd do coke left out for him."

"Did he?" she asks condescendingly. "I'm surprised because from what he told me, he didn't want you to know."

I hate her in this moment. I hate the expression of disinterest.

I hate that Evan was with her when he should have been with me.

I hate that she knew he was keeping secrets.

More than that, I despise that she has any hold over my emotions at all. How could this woman affect me so much? My inner voice hisses, *because you let her.*

"It was a mistake on his part," I lie to her, my fingers tensing as I grip my purse harder. "He got drunk one night a few weeks ago and lashed out at me. It's the last time we spoke." Her expression changes slightly, but only slightly, with a raised brow and the hint of a smirk. Amusement. I fucking hate her.

"Maybe it was a mistake to come here. I thought you'd know or maybe get a sense of how Evan's doing since you were with him."

"I have no idea what you're talking about." Leaning forward, she puts out the cigarette in a mug that's sitting on her furnace. It's then that I know she's not going to tell me a damn thing. She's far too stiff and closed off.

"My apologies for coming then," I say, shrugging it off. There's some piece of me that wants to confront her about the affair years ago. A part of me that wants to tell her I know.

She's a liar, though. It's so very clear. There isn't anything I need from this woman.

"It was a mistake on my part," I say then offer her a sad smile, taking in the room once again. "I hope you get everything you want from the divorce." I leave her with that false sincerity. The only thing I hope is that I don't have a reason to ever think of her again. She's nothing more than a waste of time and breath. Every second I've wasted on her is one I'll never get back and this woman isn't worth my time.

CHAPTER
twenty-six

Evan

"Wʜᴀᴛ'ᴅ ʏᴏᴜ ᴅᴏ ᴛᴏᴅᴀʏ?" Kᴀᴛ ᴀsᴋs ᴀs I turn on the stove, listening to the clicks before the gas lights.

"Not much," I answer her as I look over my shoulder. *Just hunting down the identity of a drug dealer.*

"What do you think you want to do?" Kat asks me as I pour olive oil into a pan. Chicken marsala for dinner. My throat goes dry as I remember how Pops taught me how to cook it; it was one of his favorites.

"Like do for work?" I ask to clarify and put the chicken in the pan. The sizzle is perfect.

She shrugs and hops up on the counter, setting her ass down and letting her feet dangle. "I know you have some investments."

"'Some' is putting it lightly. If you're worried about money, don't be. We'll be fine." I haven't checked in a week or two on some of the stocks, but the savings account is more than enough. We've been here so long, both of us working and not doing much of anything else, the money piled up. "I promise we'll be fine, baby. You don't have to worry about that."

"I'm not really worried about money, it's more about what you're going to do with yourself." She's kept her distance in an odd way I haven't experienced before. She's careful with me. Every question seems planned, every touch cautious. It's obvious that she's still scared.

I flip the breasts over and pick up the pan, making sure to spread the oil before setting it back down. Just like how Pops used to do.

"We have a baby coming and you want to move," I answer her and stride over, my bare feet padding on the floor as I go. Standing between her legs with my hands resting lightly on her hips, I tell her, "That's all I've been thinking about for now."

There's a small hesitation before she speaks and a tension that flashes between us. *That and James.* His name is always on the tip of my tongue for any conversation we have. The threat of him lingers, even though we pretend it doesn't.

"The baby won't be here for a while," she finally says and threads her fingers through my hair. I love it when she does this. When she loves on me. I missed this. "I'm worried about you," she adds and I back away slightly, but she keeps me there, tightening her legs around me.

"Don't be upset," she says and her tone begs me to listen.

"I'm fine," I respond stiffly and even I know it's a lie.

"You just lost your father, and …"

"Stop worrying about me."

"You scared me last night with the night terror. And the ones you've had before," she adds.

"It'll be over soon," I reassure her and get back to cooking. "I have sleeping pills and that's going to help." It's quiet for a moment, but that doesn't last long. Kat's not the best at giving up on what she wants.

"What about seeing someone?" she asks.

"What, like a shrink?"

"They aren't called shrinks," she says, reprimanding me. Some days I think she thinks it's all in my head. Like maybe I'm crazy.

"I'll see one. I promise." It's on my to-do list. It's just at the very bottom of it for now.

The tension clears as I reach for the Italian mix of spices. With just a pinch of cayenne.

"Thank you," she whispers and before I can respond, she asks again, "So what do you *want* to do?" At least she moved on from talking about Pops, the nightmares, and seeing a professional about all the shit going on in my head.

Peering back at her and wiping my hands with a kitchen towel, I note the devotion in her gaze. It'd bother me, if I didn't know how damn much she loves and needs me.

"I'm not worried about keeping myself busy."

She purses her lips and nods, but she doesn't seem convinced.

"I'm going to be fine," I say and stir the sauce before layering it onto the cooked chicken.

She murmurs in that sweet voice of hers, "You better be."

"You know what I'm going to do?" I ask her as I continue cooking and ignore the sick feeling in the pit of my stomach about everything *currently* going on. "I'm going to move us out of here and into our forever home. I promise," I say, and she rolls her eyes.

"For the love of God, hire a moving company this time," she states with exasperation and I give her the laugh she's after. The move here was … something for the books.

"I'm going to find a house you love and help you make it ours." I tap the tongs on the side of the pan as I pull it off the burner and then walk back to her. "I'm going to set up our baby's room and make it perfect with all the little details."

She likes that. Kat sways on the counter like she's giddy at the thought and a genuine smile lifts up her lips. Making them that much more kissable.

"I'm going to make sure the two of you have nothing to worry about and that the three of us are happy and healthy, and all that good stuff they write about in fairytales."

She lets out a small laugh and wraps her arms around my shoulders. That's what I'm after. That's all I'm after.

"I love you, babe," I tell her, and she leans in for a small kiss.

"I love you too … I just hate seeing you anything other than happy."

"I'll be better when this is over with," I say, bringing up the one thing I don't want to speak about. She kisses me soft and sweet, and it feels right. She's a balm to my soul, but it doesn't take the pain away.

She doesn't release me like I think she will. Instead she holds on tighter.

"I'm worried about you," she whispers against my lips.

I brush my nose against hers. "It's not supposed to work that way."

Her green eyes peek up at me through her thick lashes and she says, "Yeah it is. It works both ways. Don't you know that by now?"

CHAPTER
twenty-seven

Kat

"I THOUGHT WE WERE JUST GOING TO ORDER out," Evan says from across the table. The silverware clinks in his hand as he picks up the white cloth napkin and lays it on his lap.

The Savinga Grill has always been one of my favorite restaurants since I first discovered it years ago. With exposed dark red brick, raw wood beams, and high ceilings, it's rustic, it's cozy, and it's only a cab ride away.

That's what I told Evan to get him here when he asked where I wanted to go. *Just a cab ride away.*

I shrug and say, "I wanted to go out."

"It makes me nervous," he tells me. I know it does. I realize this is a risk and one he didn't want to take, but time is not on our side and I've waited long enough.

I lay my hand on the table, palm up, and wait for him to take it. "Mason said you need to be seen."

"Me, not *us*." He emphasizes the word "us."

"It's part of us moving forward together." The smile on my lips is small but it's still there. "I won't let someone keep me from you or us from our lives."

His lips twitch with a response, but he doesn't say anything. Two weeks have passed since I told him we were pregnant. Two weeks came and went, and I'm officially in our second trimester now.

"We tried this your way, now we try it mine," I tell him, and my words come out hard.

"And your way is to go out and risk being seen?"

"I want us to go out, yes … like we used to." My answer is blunt as I pull my napkin across my lap. "I'm not going to hide away in some dark room and let my fear cripple me." My voice is stern but also sympathetic. "If someone wants to know if we're together, let them know." He woke up last night with sweat pouring down his face. He was screaming in his sleep. I refuse to play this psychological game. I'm going to be there for my husband. I'm going to do everything I can to make him better. And that means not hiding and not being scared.

I'll be strong for him. I'll be strong for us both. At this point I don't know what to think of his ex-boss or how Tony died. I know my husband is letting his fear kill him, though. It's shoved itself between us and I can't let that happen anymore. He refuses to go to the cops. He's not ready to see a psychologist. I'm okay with that, but I'm not okay with nothing changing for the better.

"I won't let a single person keep us from moving on with our lives. That means being together and going to my favorite restaurant to celebrate."

I flash him a smile as the waiter walks over to us. Like this conversation doesn't put me on edge.

It's quiet while the water is being poured, and stays that way except for the waiter informing us of the specials and handing us a pair of menus.

It's only when he leaves us that I continue what I was saying.

"Yes, I want us to be seen. I also want to celebrate being pregnant. I want to buy a new house, a bigger one closer to the park." My fingertips play along the stem of the water goblet and I rest my elbow on the table as I talk while reading the menu, even though I already know what I want. "I want to slow down with work and I want the world to know it all. I want to move forward, Evan. I want everything that happened to stay in the past."

He only responds with a tight smile.

"I'm not going to let this change us and who we are."

"I don't want you to be in danger," he answers me, leaning back in his seat and casually glancing to his left and right. I recognize a man sitting alone a few tables away. Occasionally he glances up at us. It was Evan's concession and I allow it.

"Too late, baby," I say and my smile falters.

"I feel uncomfortable being here," he says and guilt digs its claws into me at his admission. I'm trying to do what's right. That's all I want to do.

"I feel like"—taking a deep inhale, I steady myself to

continue, meeting his concerned gaze—"like you're per-petuating your fears by hiding away and only focusing on them. Not just focusing, but allowing them to dictate everything." My voice cracks with the confession. I have to take another sip of water to calm myself down. "I hate that you're constantly on edge when we leave the house."

"You don't understand," he tells me with a frustrated sigh that pisses me off.

"It felt like you'd died when you left me," I say. "So, I think I do understand." I take another drink of water and ask, "What if the cops stop looking into what happened? They have no leads." I stress the basic truth. "What if James gets away with it all? What then? Will you carry on like this?"

He doesn't answer, although I can see his will to fight me has left.

"I just want us back," I say. "That's really what it comes down to."

This time it's Evan who puts his hand on the table and I'm more than happy to reach for him. He kisses my knuckles then my wrist. "I'm sorry," he whispers against my racing pulse.

"I know you are, but what am I?" I give him a joking response to lighten the mood and it works somewhat.

As Evan's lips pull into a smile and he relaxes his posture, he takes my hand in his.

"You know I miss this side of you?" he tells me.

"What side?"

"The playful side," he answers and squeezes my hand … kind of like how my heart squeezes. This is the version of my husband I want all the time. The man I know and love.

"Can I tell you a secret?" I whisper just before the waiter walks up to us. "I miss it too."

"Are you two ready to order?" the waiter asks, looking between us and clasping his hands in front of him.

"You first," Evan says and gestures at me.

"The lasagna please, with a house salad." I almost order a glass of cabernet but then I stop myself. Every time I remember we're having a baby, it's a gift in itself.

"I'll have the same," Evan says, and it surprises me.

When the waiter leaves, I comment with a questioning smirk, "You never have lasagna."

He shrugs and says, "I guess I want to try it your way."

"We have the next doctor's appointment coming up and since you're no longer working, I assume you're coming with me?"

"Of course," Evan says then nods and leans forward, lowering his voice and adding a huskiness to it that makes every inch of my body tingle. "You know you look beautiful, right?"

I can't help the smile and blush that spread across my face at his compliment. "Stop," I say, brushing him off.

"Never," he answers playfully, his handsome asymmetric smile toying with my emotions.

That warm cheery feeling in my chest slowly drifts away as I remember my own little secret. Not so little, really.

"I have something to tell you," I say, uttering the words even at the risk of upsetting Evan. I guess I waited intentionally for us to be out in public before I could tell him. "I did something that I don't think you're going to like."

"What's that?" he asks easily, although I notice his shoulders stiffen.

"I was curious about something and I think it's something only I would know how to ask appropriately …"

I don't know how to word this, and I find myself staring at the ice in the glass of water.

"You can tell me. Whatever it is."

"I went to see Samantha a couple days ago. At her place on Fifth Avenue," I tell him, confessing before I can stop myself. The air instantly changes as Evan doesn't respond. He seems uncomfortable if anything.

"I had to know for myself."

"What did you have to know?" He shifts in his seat

"I had to know if she was your type. What she was like. So I know how to react when her name comes up."

Evan runs his hand down the back of his head as he looks away from me. "Her name isn't going to come up …"

"You don't understand—" I start to explain but he cuts me off.

"There's no one else for me, Kat," he tells me bluntly, his hands hitting the table and rattling the small plates. The couple a table down from us glances in our direction and Evan grimaces. Sometimes he doesn't realize his own strength.

"I knew you would be upset—" I begin my apology and again he cuts me off.

"But you did it anyway." His cocked brow adds some humor although I still feel guilty over it all.

I nod my head once. "I did. And it's over."

The tension between us lifts a bit as I look him in the eyes and say, "It's over. There's nothing there and I'm fine now, but I had to tell you."

"You're fine?"

"Yes," I answer and I am. "There's no way she's your type."

My response gets a short laugh from Evan. A genuine smile even. "You know you're crazy?" he asks me.

"I do. And you made me this way."

"Fair enough," he says but then his expression gets serious.

"I know, don't do it again," I say before he can tell me.

"I'm serious," he says, and I nod.

I glance to Evan's right, toward the front of the restaurant as another couple walks in. "I was surprised that Samantha does pills," I say absently. More to gossip than anything else. Well, maybe to throw her under the bus a little. I can admit that I'm not a big enough woman not to.

"What?" Evan asks.

"There was coke on her kitchen table, lying out in the open." He looks back at me with an expression that's not quite disbelief, but something else.

"Coke?" he echoes. "Sam doesn't do drugs."

I ignore the fact that he called her Sam and nod my head once while I add, "And a bag of pills. She had a variety pack, Adderall and a mix of things. It was like a grab bag. I would never have guessed she does drugs." I wait for him to say something.

"Speed?" he asks me again although it's not quite spoken like a question.

"I didn't say speed," I reply.

"Adderall is speed," he tells me with a concerned expression.

"Oh, I didn't know. I don't know what they were. I just know what I saw and I was shocked. I'm just guessing it's Adderall." I swallow thickly, wishing I'd just kept my mouth shut and saved the gossip for the girls.

I watch as Evan's forehead pinches, but there's something else in his expression that catches me off guard. It's hard and unforgiving. Something that sends a chill down my spine. Even his hands clench into fists on top of the table. I glance at them and then his eyes, but movement behind him at the front of the restaurant catches my attention.

"Is that Suzette?" Even with the shock of seeing her stride in just now, I don't think I've ever been happier for a change of subject. I wish I could snatch the last two minutes of our conversation from the air and shove them back into my petty mouth.

"It's definitely Sue," I say, holding up Evan's end of this conversation since he's still silent. I'd know that blunt bob anywhere. She walks slowly as she digs in her purse, looking for something at the front of the restaurant.

I'm pushing my chair out from the table when my mouth drops open at the sight of a man coming up from behind her.

He's much taller than she is even in her heels. I don't recognize him; he's facing away from me. In a black suit, he stalks up behind her, moving his hand to her waist and pulling her close to him.

"Who is that?" I say beneath my breath, but when I look to Evan and try to get his attention, he's busy on his phone.

"Babe," I say, not so quietly trying to get his attention. It's not every day you see one of your good friends being felt up by someone you don't know. I much prefer this conversation. It's easy and Evan always has something to say about whoever Sue is "dating."

I have to turn my head when I look back up to keep my eyes on them and try to follow them down the hall. But they're gone before I even get the chance to stand.

I swear it was her and I go to reach for my phone to send her a message, but glancing at Evan, he stops me in mid reach.

"What's wrong?" I ask him as he stares at his phone.

"We have to go." His response is hard and nonnegotiable.

"We just got here," I object, but that doesn't stop him from standing up abruptly as the waiter returns to our table.

"I'm so sorry, we have to go," Evan tells the waiter. "Please cancel the order."

"Are you serious?" I hiss as the couple from before looks at us again.

"I'm sorry, but something just came up," he tells me and there's a look in his eyes that's begging me not to push him.

"Please, Kat," he says, ushering me away. "We need to leave. Now."

Evan

"This alley smells like piss," Mason says as we stop between a Chinese restaurant and a shoe store. I met up with him on Prince Street and we walked our way here. Just me and him … and business to take care of.

I take a whiff and immediately regret it. "This is where he's going, though, right?"

"Should already be there," he answers.

"That's what it said on his profile. 'Getting ready for the party,'" he elaborates beneath his breath and shoves his hands in his pockets.

It's bitterly cold and the city streets are packed with people shopping and moving about like normal.

"I don't believe in coincidences," I tell Mason and bring it up again.

His eyes flicker to me and then back across the street.

"There's no way she happens to do speed," I tell him. I've known Samantha for a long damn time. "Her husband dabbles in all sorts of drugs recreationally. But she doesn't touch it. She never has."

"It's possible she does it on the down low," he suggests. "You'd be surprised how many people do coke nowadays."

I shake my head. "There has to be a connection between her and the dealer."

"We're gonna find out, aren't we?" he asks me, although it's a rhetorical question.

"What's the plan?"

"All we need is an address."

"Just follow him, then?" I ask with disbelief.

"Only for a bit, then we switch off so we aren't seen."

"Switch off to who?"

"I got some guys," Mason says, and frustration gets the best of me.

"I want to be the one—" I start, but he's quick to cut me off.

"You want to keep her safe? Getting into this shit isn't what you need. That's not what the man who deserves to be at Kat's side would do."

That shuts me up, but I fucking hate it. He's been edging me out of this. Giving me less and less.

"So, we just wait?" I ask him again.

"Yeah," he answers, and his breath turns to fog, "just wait."

Almost an hour passes before I think about going back to Kat. She has no idea what this could mean. I'm sure she'll be pissed I took off in addition to cutting our date short. Sirens wail in the distance and the busy city night reminds me of how things used to be.

"Fuck me," I say out loud and run my hands down my face.

"Sorry, you're not my type," Mason says so matter-of-factly from his spot next to me, I grunt a short laugh despite myself. "I feel so fucking trapped."

"I know the feeling," Mason tells me, and I give him a sidelong glance. His stare only hardens. "I know what it's like to be in a lose-lose situation where the stakes are high." He looks forward, staring at the opposite brick wall in the thin alley. "Too high," he mutters under his breath.

"So, what do you do?" I say and get his attention again. "How do you win?" I ask him with complete sincerity as if he has an answer that will put an end to this hell.

He shakes his head as he looks down at the ground and replies, "Sometimes there's not a way to win, only a way to survive."

I have to tear my eyes away from him, knowing he's right and when I do, I spot something. My arm reaches out and I smack him in the chest.

"Visual." The single word is barely spoken from me, and Mason doesn't hesitate to take out his phone and call the tail. "He's here," he speaks into the phone as both of us watch the perp, chatting with some guy in an open doorway on Twentieth and Broadway. Even from his profile, I know it's him.

Every muscle in my body coils, ready to fight. It's been weeks of holding back and not being able to do anything.

And just across the street is the last piece to this puzzle of fucking misery.

Dark black hair slicked back and tanned skin with a tattoo scrolling up his neck. It's definitely him. We got this prick.

The second he's walking down the stone steps, we're moving out of the alley and following from across the street. I keep my eyes on him, walking through the thick crowd with my jaw clenched.

"Johnny, we got him." Mason talks into his cell phone as we walk. I try not to make it obvious that we're following the fucker. At the same time, I'm holding back every desire to chase the dealer down and beat the shit out of him to get every bit of information from him.

Mason says we should bribe him. It's not exactly my style, though.

"Heading down Twenty-second," I hear Mason say and instinctively I glance up to look at the street sign before turning left to follow him.

My blood's pumping hard and with every step it gets harder and harder not to pick up speed.

Right as we get to the end of the block and the crosswalk sign turns to a red hand, the fucker walks out, ignoring the oncoming cars and nearly getting hit, but he keeps going, yelling out, "Hey, watch it!" at the drivers as if it's their fault. I move to do the same. We can't risk losing him, but Mason puts his arm out in front of my chest to stop me.

"He's got him," he tells me, his eyes glued to the dealer's back as he vanishes into the thick crowd. "Johnny's on him."

My shoulders rise and fall with my heavy breaths. I'm calm on the outside, but inside I'm pacing. The nerves eat away at me. "I need to do something," I tell him, ignoring how the woman to my right turns back to look at me as if I've lost it. Maybe I have.

"Then go home," Mason says and turns halfway around to walk right back up the way we came.

His leather jacket bunches in my fist as I pull him back to me. "I can't sit around and do nothing," I say, pleading with him to understand.

"The best thing for you to do is go home to your pregnant wife and stay right the fuck there," Mason tells me. That's it? That's all I can do when this is the prick that laced that coke? When he's the one who sold the tainted version and he's the only one who can tell us who he sold it to.

I swallow thickly, feeling guilt settle in my stomach. "She needs you to be there," Mason asserts, with caution thick in every word. I wonder if he's just saying that to make me listen to his order, or if he really means it.

"You told her you were done with this shit. Be done with it. You saw him, you know we got the guy. It's just a matter of time now."

CHAPTER
twenty-nine

Kat

EVAN IS ... NOT HIMSELF IN THE LEAST. His shoulders are hunched, and he keeps checking his phone like he's waiting for something.

Ever since we left dinner last night, he's been closed off. I wish I'd never brought up Samantha. It was a mistake.

Evan checks his phone again as an explosion on the television booms through the living room. He doesn't flinch or react. He's numb.

I scroll through the list I've added to the baby registry. Maddie sent me a check-off chart and it's so, so long. All the clothes in miniature and every odd and end, from pacifier holders to little mittens, should be enjoyable to add, but there's a nagging feeling that claws at my chest.

I peek up at him again, scooting closer into the

cushion and pulling the throw tighter around me. "Why do you keep checking your phone?"

"It's nothing," he answers.

I'm slow and deliberate as I arrange myself into a cross-legged position across from my husband on the sofa.

The expression on his face is one I've seen before, the "what is she doing?" look.

He sets his phone down beside him, and I don't take my eyes off his, but I notice how he tries to hide it.

"No secrets," I remind him. "You promised."

Another loud boom from the television distracts me and I reach for the remote without hesitation, bending over Evan to grab it from where it sits right next to his phone. As soon as the television screen goes black, I toss the remote behind me.

Giving him my full attention I tell him, "I feel like maybe you have something to tell me." I hold his gaze and his expression gives me nothing.

I'm so close to snatching his phone out of his hands just to prove him wrong, but before I pull the trigger on that idea he says, "I don't want to bother you with these things."

"You're my husband. You're supposed to bother me." I say it with a little humor, but again, he doesn't react.

"Tell me, Evan. I *want* to know." I scoot closer to him, just a bit so my leg touches his and I rest a hand on his thigh.

"It's something you said. About Samantha having drugs." Dread washes over me. I never should have gone to see her, confront her or spoken her name. I regret it all.

He glances away from me at the far wall in the room. "It's something bad," he adds.

"Her having drugs is … what? I don't understand." I hate that an inkling of jealousy creeps up on me, but it's quickly followed by a darker realization. The coldness that came with the dread sinks down deeper, coating every inch of my skin.

"The coke that killed Tony was laced with another drug. High amounts, enough to kill." He looks me in the eye and slowly the pieces come together, one by one.

A chill sinks into the marrow of my bones. Samantha. Not James. "Did you tell Mason?"

He nods and then adds, "He thinks he has something concrete."

"What?" I ask him, eager for more. I can't lie. There's a part of me that's afraid, but a bigger part that needs to know. Ever since Evan told me his theory, I've questioned it. I've questioned his sanity even. I started to think it was all in his head.

"He can't tell me over the phone," Evan says as if that's the end of the discussion.

"Is it good or bad?" I ask him, guilt and stupidity both weighing down my words.

"Good, I think." He hesitates, but then adds, "He said it's done and to come see him. I'm just waiting for the time and place."

"It's done?" I question, feeling my eyes widen with hope. My lungs stay perfectly still until Evan nods his head once.

"Just waiting for the time and place." He turns his

attention back to the television and then glances at the remote.

There's an eerie feeling that settles between us, a darkness I can't seem to grasp.

"You know I love you, right?" he asks as he brushes the hair out of my face.

My eyes flicker from his chest to his eyes as I say, "I do."

His lips twitch into a smile and he leans forward to kiss me. It's chaste and quick, but he rests his forehead against mine, his hand still on my jaw.

"I don't like this," he whispers.

I can't respond. The words are caught in my throat and I have nothing to say other than, "I love you too. I'll wait with you."

CHAPTER
thirty

Evan

I STARE DOWN AT THE PAPER AND THEN LOOK BACK to Mason. I've known since Kat told me. Samantha's the reason that coke was laced, and it wasn't meant for me at all. It was James she wanted dead. I'm a fucking fool.

Anger rolls through me like a low tide. Slowly rising and each wave threatening to take more and more of me away.

"She was fucking him," Mason says.

"Fucking who?" Kat asks, still clinging to my side. With my arm around her, I pull her in closer. She insisted on coming and at first, I didn't want her here. I didn't want to involve her in this more than I already had.

Now though, knowing she went to Samantha, that she spoke to her, and was inside her apartment, so close to a woman capable of murder, I need her here with me.

She's not allowed to leave my side until this is finished.

I rub soothing circles along her hip as I look past Mason and out through the picture window in his sitting room. I need to feel her. I need to know she's still here, alive and by my side. Away from any danger.

"Samantha was fucking Andrew, the dealer. They planned to kill James and it went sideways. He was supposed to do the coke, not give it to Evan to share with Tony."

"Do you have evidence?" Kat asks, and I look down at her. She's standing there as if she just asked for a receipt for an item she wants to return to Nordstrom, not at all affected in the least.

"Enough of it," Mason answers and I look back at him when I can feel his eyes on me. "Shots of her with Andrew taken from his own surveillance feed. You can't tell it's him, since it's his back and he's wearing a hoodie. More importantly, my guy was able to grab a sample."

We can plant the tainted coke. That's easy enough. Send the picture anonymously to Detective Bradshaw, plant the coke and boom, there's the evidence they've been after. There's the matter of what she'll say when they come for her, though. Who she'll blame and throw under the bus.

The details still need to be decided, but the truth is there. Now we know what happened.

"She wanted James dead because the divorce wasn't going to leave her with anything?" Kat asks Mason and he's quick to respond.

"She's the one who cheated and according to their

prenup, if we go by the gossip columns, a divorce would leave her without a penny to her name."

"Better to kill him than to finalize the divorce," Kat comments under her breath and steps away from me, walking to the far side of the room to pick up the cup of hot tea she left on the side table.

"What about James?" I ask him. "He really had nothing to do with this?"

Mason shrugs. "Still a prick, and now he's onto his wife because of the nudge we gave him, but I don't have shit on him."

I break eye contact and wipe a hand down my face. I feel like a fool. Guilt and regret swirl together, and the mix of emotions makes me numb. I have to remind myself that all I need right now is Kat, just my wife.

"You were wrong," Kat says from across the room.

"I wanted to kill him … I would have," I admit to them, and it hurts to do it. The past few nights I've lain awake, thinking about all the ways I considered murdering him. As I stood outside of his house, I knew it'd be easy. I craved to see his body lifeless on the floor.

"It's because of her," Kat speaks lowly, but her breathing picks up as anger gets the best of her.

"It's not hard to focus on revenge," Mason says as if reading my mind. "It's not your fault for wanting this over so you could protect your wife."

The clink of ceramic on glass gets my attention as Kat sets down her mug and makes her way back to me.

"So, what do we do now?" Kat asks then leans her back against my front.

Mason smirks at her and looks between the two of us. "See, this I love," he says, tapping the folder in his hands.

"We came up with a plan. The cops have to find out. James and Samantha need to be focused on each other and forget about me."

"So … what's the plan? Leak it to them somehow?" Kat questions.

Mason steps in and says, "James is going to post about how Samantha's fucking a drug dealer. He's going to write all about how he found coke and a grab bag of pills in her office and that's why they've split."

"How do you know that?"

"Because my guy has access to his email account. And he drugged him about two hours ago. James is going to wake up with a hangover and unleash hell when he realizes he emailed his contact at the *News Journal*, who's eager to post anything at all about this case.

"The cops are itching for something and they know they have nothing. This city talks, and Derek at the *News Journal* will foam at the mouth to have the inside scoop before anyone else," Mason answers Kat.

I hope it's enough to satisfy her. She can't know the last piece. Just one more secret. One final release.

"James will be relieved more than anything else," I add, trying to ease her worry. "He's a time bomb of paranoia waiting to go off." Mason backs up, leaning against the back of a sitting chair as he adds, "And Samantha will be behind bars by morning."

"She can't deny the pictures of the evidence," Kat murmurs, grasping the plan, but quickly licks her lower lip and shakes her head, seemingly finding a gap in the details. "She'll make bail."

"With the cops James has in his back pocket?" Mason looks at her with disbelief. "No way. She's done." He's good at convincing her this will work, even though I'm still not convinced. If anything, I know nothing is bulletproof.

A moment passes and I let my hand slip to the small of her back. It takes everything in me to assure her, "It's done. This will work and it's done." There's a nagging feeling in the pit of my stomach, knowing either one of them could mention my name. I could go down too. But it's a risk I have to take for all this to be over. I can't outrun it and I'm willing to take a deal, I'm willing to do anything to put an end to it all.

"Good," Kat says with finality.

"Do you need me to do anything?" I ask Mason as Kat cradles her body against mine.

"I can take it from here, but I'd stay inside and keep a low profile until there's word about the arrest."

I give him a tight smile then lean down to kiss Kat's hair, savoring every moment. I'm doing it for her. With my throat tight and everything inside me ringing, I whisper, "Let's go home, baby."

One week later

"Is he in there?" I ask Mason as we sit in the car.

Andrew Jones, also known as Mathew Staller, is about to meet his maker. The man who sold Samantha the drugs, helped her plan a murder, and got off with nothing has to pay for what he's done.

He didn't get a single charge that stuck to him. Not a damn thing. Samantha protected him and pled guilty when it came down on her. So did James, accepting the weaker charges that were merely slaps on the wrists. I slipped under the radar, although I'm certain Mason had something to do with that.

Andrew got off completely. Until now.

"Yeah, this is his address," Mason answers as he unbuckles his seatbelt. The click is loud in the still night air.

I watch the light at the end of the street turn green, but there's not a single car down the road where Andrew's house is. Not a person in sight, in fact.

It's only him and us.

I guess he liked being out here for his privacy, away from the city in a Podunk area … maybe it's where he cooks up the drugs. Or maybe he's lying low since it all went down only days ago.

I don't know, and I don't give a fuck. All I want is for every person responsible to pay the price.

As I step out of the car, the chill of the evening creeping into my bones, I tell Mason, "You better never tell Kat."

He grins at me and says, "It's our secret."

The doors to the car close softly, although they cause

a gentle thud to resonate in the bitter cold. I keep my gaze on the warm yellow light coming from the upstairs of the two-story house.

"Sticking to the plan?"

I nod at Mason's question, not stopping my pace, and not taking my eyes off the light upstairs. Duct tape and rope are in the trunk.

I crack my knuckles one by one, all the pent-up anger and fear from the past couple of weeks raging through my blood, begging for revenge.

I came so close to losing everything because of this fucker. My wife would have been a pregnant widow. And it's because of this asshole.

"Yeah, stick to the plan," I answer Mason.

He grins at me. "I'll get the front, you get the back."

Just as we break, the man of the hour walks right out the front door, hoodie on and straight out onto the sidewalk, only feet from the car.

"I don't do meets here, get the fuck out," he informs us with a threatening tone that only heats the rage coursing in my blood.

"Not here?" Mason questions as if we're here to buy or sell or whatever the hell Andrew thinks we're here for.

"Yeah, like I said, I don't do meets here," Andrew repeats and then opens his coat, flashing a gun tucked in his waistband. "So get the fuck out."

Dumb prick should have had the gun in his hand.

The rage turns my vision red.

Before I know what I'm doing, I go for the first punch, slamming my fist right in his jaw. It's reckless, but it's a damn good release of all the tension I've been carrying. My blood rushes in my ear as he and Mason both fumble for the gun. Mason grabs it from him as a bullet goes off, flying through the air and ricocheting off the car. Crouching down, I get in another punch, stunning the dealer. It's cold and the freezing air bites into my white-knuckled fist. Over and over I feel my muscles tighten, gripping onto his collar, then letting the rage pour out of me, blow by blow. My teeth grind against one another as I don't hold back a damn thing.

Crack! The prick's jaw snaps and I feel the bones crunch under the weight of my fist. I see the images that haunted me for weeks.

Andrew pulls back his arm and lands a single solid punch to my cheek. It'll bruise, but it barely affects me. Nothing can pull me from this haze of vengeance. My head snaps to the side as another punch lands on my chin. I throw all my weight forward, pushing him to the ground and feeling my body fall on top of his, slamming hard onto the concrete sidewalk.

"Fuck!" he screams out just as I pin him under me and throw punch after punch. His nose cracks under one of them; I don't know how many I get in. I can't stop.

"Evan!" Mason cries out, his fingers prying into my shoulders then my chest, desperately pulling me backward, but I get one more hit in that snaps Andrew's head to the side and for a moment, I think he's dead. He lies there nearly lifeless. Blood's covering his face and soaking into my knuckles. Red lays in streaks everywhere.

Andrew spits blood onto the street next to him and coughs it up as I attempt to rein in my heaving breaths.

"Snap out of it. It's not the plan." Mason repeats, "It's not the plan. This isn't the plan." There's a ringing in my ears that won't quit. One that balances out my tunnel vision and the stinging pain that shoots from the split knuckles on my hand.

When I finally catch my breath, Mason is on top of him on the ground, pinning him down. Andrew knees Mason in the stomach, desperately trying to win a losing fight. But I'm too quick, grabbing his own gun and shooting him once in his thigh.

I don't want to kill him. That's not my job to do.

He's not for me. But I'll be damned if I didn't love beating the piss out of him.

Andrew screams out in agony and Mason, still wincing and holding his gut, socks him right in the mouth.

Mason catches his breath as he slowly stands up and Andrew stares up at us, begging for mercy.

"Are you Andrew Jones?" I ask him and he hesitates to answer, so I fire a shot off right next to him.

"Yes!" he screams. "Fuck! Yes!"

I crouch down in front of him, gun still in my hand. "The same Andrew Jones that left those messages for Samantha? The ones convincing her to murder her husband?" The blood drains from his face as I talk. I'm not some dealer looking to get more turf. I'm not a cop. True fear permeates the air as the fool shakes his head. "The same Andrew Jones that gave her tainted coke so she could end his life and pay you half of what the insurance company was going to give her?"

"I don't know any Samantha ..." he tries to lie, and I

shoot off the gun again, feeling the shockwaves run up my arm. It's closer to him this time and Andrew screams out.

"He pissed himself," Mason comments and when I look, sure enough, his sweats have a dark wet ring around him. He's pathetic.

"That Andrew Jones?" I ask him.

"She wanted him dead!" he yells. "She was going to do it whether I helped her or not."

"You can tell her husband that; I'm sure he'll understand," Mason says and then tosses handcuffs at his feet. "Put those on. First your feet, then your hands."

"Please," he begs. But there's no mercy for what he's done.

It takes a good fifteen minutes to tie him up. The gagging was the hardest part.

The trunk slams shut, and the dark night seems so empty. Empty is what I needed, though. It's done and over.

Mason turns the car on, the keys jingling in the ignition before it roars to life and we leave in silence, listening to the fucker in the back. It's already starting to snow. They're calling for ten inches and that will wash away any evidence of us being here. Not that anyone will come looking for a while. Like he told us, he doesn't do meets here.

My heartbeat slows, and the end feels so fucking close. Every loose end is finally being resolved.

"Thanks for doing this," I tell Mason, ignoring Andrew's muted thumps in the trunk as we go over a speed bump and then another.

"No problem." His nonchalant response is as if I've only thanked him for picking up milk on the way home.

"I just needed to do something about it all." I feel the need to explain. We could have let Mason's guy take care of him. I needed some kind of part in seeing this through, even if I promised Kat I'd stay out of it. It's the last secret and I'm done. One last deal to see through.

"It's not like he doesn't have it coming to him."

I nod at Mason's comment and listen to Andrew's muffled screams.

"You sure he's going to be here?" Mason asks me as we pull up to a vacant lot.

Even as the car slows, I can see James inside, moving aside a curtain in the bedroom.

"Yeah, I'm sure," I tell him.

I know James is here. He's waiting for sentencing and not going anywhere near the city. *He's hiding.*

I know what that's like.

"You ready?" Mason asks me, and I nod once again. "Let's do this."

We'll leave Andrew bound and gagged on James's porch. And the hard copy photos James kept of me are already in my possession.

It's a truce of sorts. I give him his final piece, he gives me mine.

More than likely he won't see a day in jail and half his charges were already dismissed. His wife is sentenced to prison for life, his worries behind him. All but the drug dealer. He was foaming at the mouth to get him.

It was an easy call to make.

Andrew's slamming every which way, but it's 4:00 a.m. in the suburbs. There isn't another house for nearly half a mile. Even if I took the gag out of his lying mouth, there's no one here but us and James.

James is right there in the doorway, rifle ready.

"Just leave him here," I tell Mason and we let Andrew drop to the ground with a muffled scream piercing the air. "James will take him from here."

With the cold air blowing in my face and the city skyline lighting up the dark night, I finally relax into the leather seat. The bite of pain that hovers over every cracked knuckle is all that's left of what happened. It'll heal and my life will go on.

I'm done now. It's all done.

It's just me and Kat now. Just the two of us.

No. The three of us.

"Do you think he told the cops anything to try to get a lighter sentence?" I ask Evan as the newspaper in my hand rustles.

Samantha pled guilty to multiple attempted murder charges and got life in prison.

James pleaded guilty to his charges as well, but his sentence is nothing compared to hers even though they found him complicit in his client's death. It's rumored that he gave up information to cut a deal. He'll be out of jail in a year or less according to what the rumor mills are saying. The dealer got off scot-free and now people are saying he skipped town in case more evidence comes in.

"Told them what exactly?" He doesn't look back at me.

Instead he lifts a picture frame off the wall of his parents' dining room. He considers it for a moment before wrapping a handful of bubble wrap around it like he has the others.

The moving company is going to be here tomorrow, but Evan wanted to box up the pictures and a few other things himself. The *valuable things* is what he told me when we left this morning. All he's packed up so far are pictures and I wish I could steal the pain away that reflects back in the glass as I catch his gaze.

"That you were there," I say, whispering the words quietly as if it's a dark secret no one can ever know. "With Tony," I add. A part of me thinks it's just too easy. I can't shake it just yet. I can't quite grasp that I get to have my happily ever after with Evan.

He shrugs a heavy shoulder and then looks me in the eyes, gauging my reaction as he lowers the wrapped picture into the box. "He doesn't have a reason to say anything. He wanted Samantha to go down, and we made that happen." His lips are pressed into a thin line as he makes his way around the table to pull out the chair next to mine.

"You really want to talk about this?" he asks me.

I glance at the article and him, swallowing my words and not knowing how to feel. The entire situation makes me uncomfortable. Worse than that … dreadful. "I want to know it's going to be okay." I offer him the truth. "I want to make sure *you're* going to be okay."

Evan smirks at me then leans forward, kissing the tip of my nose, which makes me close my eyes. "You're cute, you know that?"

I love how at ease he is. It feels like I have my husband back. Truly. Yet I'm still waiting for the other shoe to drop.

Reaching up, I quickly grab his hand and keep him close to me. "I'm serious," I say as I look him in the eyes. "I want to know you're okay."

"Baby, I told you there's nothing to worry about." He brushes his hand against my cheek, forcing me to let go. Evan pinches my chin between his thumb and forefinger, and stares into my eyes. There's a look there that makes me all warm and fuzzy. He's always been able to do that, and I love him for it.

"You promise?" I ask him softly and he pecks my lips once, then goes in for a deeper one before answering me.

"Well, we do have a baby coming," he says, still staring at my lips. "So, I'm sure we've got some things to be worried about, but that mess is over."

The stir of desire drifts away, dissolving instantly when I peek back down at the article. The picture they chose is one of Samantha giving James a death stare as she was arrested. The papers paint her as the villain she is.

"And you got that package too," Evan comments, bringing my attention back to him. My heart flickers once, then twice as I bite my lip and shrug.

"It was really nice of him," Evan says, and I feel the need to smack his arm playfully as he stands up to keep packing.

I place a hand on my belly and tell him, "It was a goodbye and good luck gift from a friend."

"A friend you kissed," Evan reminds me.

"A friend who was there for me when you weren't," I point out.

His shoulders stiffen a little as he stops midway from taking another photo off the wall. "I know," he says beneath his breath.

"It was a nice gift, though, wasn't it?" I ask him. Evan looks at me with an eyebrow raised and I have to laugh. "He doesn't have our new address anyway and he didn't put his on the package either."

"Yeah, yeah, yeah," Evan says.

"I really like it." I shrug my shoulders and remember the gift box Jake sent. Inside was a baby book called *I'll Love You Forever*. I can't read it without crying. All the note said was that he gave a copy to all his friends who were expecting and he didn't feel right not giving me one. One last kindness.

"It was nice of him, but it better be the last of him," Evan warns me jokingly. I love the trace of a smile on his lips. He knows I'm all his.

I lean back in the chair, and a yawn escapes before I can stop it. I'm halfway to telling him off in some way or another, but the words are stopped.

"You ready to go home?" he asks me and I nod my head, but add, "Only if you're all done."

He takes a look around the half-packed house and shakes his head. I have to admit watching him cleaning up his father's place makes my heart ache for him. I know I can't take the pain away. It'll always be there.

"You know our baby is going to be tough, right?" he comments just as the emotions start to get the best of me.

I rub my swollen bump in smooth circles as I pray our baby is okay in there and doesn't know how sad I am in this moment. I only want love for him or her.

"I hope so," I whisper as Evan comes back over to me. He wraps his arms around my shoulders and pulls me into his chest. I'm more than grateful as I wrap my arms around him and my cheek presses against his shirt.

"It's true. When a mom goes through hell during pregnancy and handles it as well as you have, the baby can handle anything, you know?"

I let out a sad but genuine laugh into his shirt and try to calm myself down as he rubs my back.

I peek up at him and smile as his lips touch mine.

"Everything's behind us," he adds.

I feel the need to remind him, "There's good behind us too, isn't there?"

"So much good," he says and then kisses me again before splaying his hand on my belly. "And so much more to come."

epilogue

Kat

Little blips, they come and go,
In rhythm and in time.
Black lines that paint a picture,
And soft lullabies in rhyme.
You're everything, and the reason I need,
To love and to forgive.
My only wish is to keep you safe,
For as long as I shall live.

SEEING THAT LITTLE BLIP MAKES IT REAL. "I can see his heartbeat."

"You're still convinced it's a boy?" Evan says although he doesn't take his eyes off the monitor. A trace of a smile is on his lips and it only grows when the little one moves.

"We'll find out soon," I tell him with a little more glee in my voice.

"Soon as in right now," the doctor comments, breaking up our little moment. With Evan to my right, I hold his hand as I lie back on the white paper, hearing it rustle under me. Dr. Harmony holds the wand right above my belly button. My belly is covered in clear gel and there's more than a little bump now that I'm twenty weeks along.

I'm quiet as the sound of a steady heartbeat comes through the speaker. *Lub-dub, lub-dub, lub-dub.* The only thing that distracts me for a moment is Evan placing his second hand over our joined one.

"Our little baby," he whispers in awe.

"Your little *boy*," the doctor corrects him, pointing to the screen. She keeps the wand there for a moment, tapping on the keyboard to take photos before removing the wand and the soft, rhythmic heartbeats are gone. But I heard them, I heard that steady heartbeat and that sound will stay with me forever.

"He's healthy?" Evan questions and my heart swells.

"Perfectly healthy," Dr. Harmony says as she wipes down the equipment and tosses the paper towels into the trash.

"I'll be back in just a bit with some pictures for you two." The young blond doctor has a pretty smile; it's one that reaches her eyes.

"Thank you," Evan and I say in unison.

"A boy," I murmur to him before he cuts me off with a kiss.

"We're going to have a son," Evan says, running a hand down his face. "It's real."

"Does it feel real to you now?"

Evan takes my hand again and kisses my knuckles before nodding his head.

My gaze moves from Evan to the screen. The little heart is beating in a perfect rhythm.

"I have a feeling it's going to be really, really good," I tell him and get a little choked up.

"It is," Evan says and kisses my hand once more. "I know it is."

Evan

The morning brings a bright light,
Hope and laughter too.
And with time comes a new love,
Faded dreams become anew.
Just remember to hold tight,
And fight for what you love.
For our lost ones will watch over,
And keep us safe from up above.

"We should name him Henry," Kat suggests as we walk into the house. The homes near the Manhattan Bridge are an expensive area to live, but the park is close, and this school district is where Kat wants to live for our little one, so how could I say no?

She tosses the keys onto the side table, walking past a row of cardboard boxes and a stack of dishes I brought back from the old place last night. "I've thought a lot about it. And I think we should."

"Henry." I say my father's name and a swell of unexpected emotion catches me off guard. I slip the jacket off my shoulders and move to busy myself, opening the window in the dining room and ignoring the look Kat gives me.

"I know it hasn't been a long time since he passed," Kat says. "It feels like it was yesterday."

She holds her swollen abdomen and drags out the head chair in the dining room. At least this room is mostly put together. Kat's nesting has her up all hours and doing shit she shouldn't do. Like carrying heavy boxes and climbing on the furniture to hang curtains. She's ever the stubborn one.

"I wish he were here with us," she murmurs and gets teary eyed; she's been crying a lot more recently, probably due to the third trimester pregnancy hormones. "But we can give him this, you know?"

Her voice is tight with emotion and I nod my head, understanding what she's saying but not wanting to voice it.

The wind blows through the house. It's warm for late March. The breeze gently moves the napkins on the table so I'm quick to tuck them into the holder and attempt to form a response. I miss my father. More than I ever could have imagined.

"He'd have loved to help us move down here." I say the thought out loud to offer her something.

"At least this time you hired movers," Kat says with a bit of humor, but her voice is solemn.

She winces with pain and grabs ahold of her belly, her eyes closed tight and my heart races.

"Babe?" She ignores me, just like she's been doing. For some unknown reason, I continue to think she'll respond during these Braxton-Hicks contractions.

Hovering over her, I eye her carefully then walk slowly to her and wait, afraid to do anything wrong.

I may have made mistakes while learning to be a good husband, but Pops showed me how to be a good father and I won't let him down.

"Oh my gosh, that was a long one." Kat finally breathes out as her body visibly relaxes.

"Do you want to go in?" My nerves are all on edge. I'm terrified, but I won't tell Kat. I've never even held a child, let alone having one depend on me to live.

Kat rolls her eyes at me. "For one contraction? I think not."

She reaches into the bag at her feet and pulls out a water bottle. "Besides, I read a baby comes when you're ready and relaxed, and we have four more rooms to set up and get settled in before I'll be anywhere near relaxed. And another two weeks until our due date."

A huff of humor leaves me and I move the top box off the nearest stack, ripping the tape back to expose what's inside.

"So, what do you think?" she asks me.

"About what?"

"About naming him Henry?" She tilts her head to the side and her long hair falls over her shoulder.

"I think Pops would have loved that," I say, getting out

the answer before my throat goes tight and take in a deep breath. "I think he'd be proud."

Lowering myself to the floor in front of her, I let my hands rest on her thighs and bring my forehead down to rest on her belly. "What do you think?" I ask our son and Kat's belly shakes as she laughs.

"You think it's funny, but he's going to know my voice." Kat doesn't hesitate to lean down and kiss me. The first one is a peck on my cheek, but then she moves her hand to my jaw and keeps me still for a longer one, a deeper one.

It's slow and sensual and makes my blood heat.

"I know he will, and I love you for it."

I take her small hand in mine and look deep into her eyes. She's seen so much of me. All of my bad along with the little bit of good I have in me, and she still loves me. There's no way I could doubt that. "I know this past year has been rough, but I'm going to do everything I can to make our lives easy for … forever."

A small smile seems to tickle Kat's lips, still a darker hue from our kiss, and she moves her fingers to them.

"I mean it, Kat. I love you and this baby more than anything." Tears come to my eyes and I only pray she knows that I love her just as much as she loves me.

After a moment, she nods. "I know you do, and I know you will."

Moving my hand to her belly, I feel our little one kick just beneath the small bit of pressure. It still gets me every time.

"He knows too," Kat says with a smile that lights her eyes.

"So, Henry?" I question, feeling a swell of pride in my chest.

She nods her head, her eyes getting glossy as she puts a hand on her belly.

"Henry."

Diary Entry Three

Hey Pops,

I wanted you to know, every day I think about what I should do to make you proud. Even the days I mess up. I guess those days especially. Your voice is always there, telling me to make it right.

Lately, I've been doing good. I think you'd agree. Sometimes I make mistakes. Like when little Henry peed through his diaper last week at four in the morning. I changed his diaper but didn't change the onesie. Kat let me have it for that one.

Common sense and all that goes out the window when it comes to him. She didn't tell me to change the onesie too. I should have known, but I'm just so careful around him. She's teaching me, though, and we're learning together. You'd love it. We miss you so much.

He's so small, Pops, I can hold him in one hand. I'm scared I'm gonna break him some days. Kat tells me I'm fine, and that I look good holding him. But I'm terrified I'm going to mess up.

I guess I'm just nervous to ruin it, so I keep waiting for her to tell me what to do.

She's taking good care of me. Especially in that department.

She's not going to mess up and that's the only thing that makes me think it's all going to be all right.

Kat's not gonna let me get away with anything anymore.

The best part about that is that I love it.

I wish I'd listened to you sooner, Pops. I want you to know, I'm trying to make sure my marriage is like yours and Ma's.

I've got to go. I just really wanted to talk to you tonight. Some nights are harder than others and I'm not sure it'll ever get too easy. Even if it does, I'll be thinking of you and wanting your advice.

I love you. We all do.

ABOUT THE
author

Thank you so much for reading my romances. I'm just a stay at home mom and avid reader turned author and I couldn't be happier.

I hope you love my books as much as I do!

More by Willow Winters
www.WillowWintersWrites.com/books